NIGHT OF THE WOLF MOON

NEW WORLD SHIFTERS
BOOK ONE

KIMBERLY LOTH

NINA WALKER

NIGHT OF THE WOLF MOON

NEW WOLF SHIFTERS BOOK ONE

KIMBERLY LOTH

NINA WALKER

Cover designed by MiblArt.

Edited by Ailene Kubricky

And Cookie Lynn Publishing

Paperback ISBN 978-1-950093-29-8

Hardcover ISBN 978-1-950093-30-4

Paperback & Hardcover Editions

Published by Addison & Grey Press

CHAPTER 1

FOURTEEN MINUTES.

It seems a trivial amount of time—but had I been born fourteen minutes earlier—I'd be the claimed one instead of my sister.

"It's going to be okay," I whisper in Willow's ear and tighten our hug even though I know it won't be. Nothing will ever be okay after today. "You're stronger than anyone I know."

The soft wind blows, rustling through the cotton field behind us. We've come to the edge of the village because we don't want the wolves getting anywhere near our homes. I'm the only sibling here today, and that's because I insisted on coming. The rest of the field is sprinkled with voyeurs pretending to be supportive, three sets of parents, two claimed daughters, and one unlucky son. Mama, Willow, and I don't stand too close to the other families, or anyone, for that matter. There is no solidarity among us—we're all here because we had no choice.

Willow starts to shake, fists clenching against my back, but not because she's crying. My sister doesn't cry when she's afraid. She gets angry.

"I love you, Poppy." She steps back, practically peeling us apart, and addresses Mama and me one last time. "Goodbye."

Only I can see the slight tremble in her limbs that indicates that she's on the verge of losing her courage.

She turns her back on us and marches across the barren field toward the other two claimed, Charlotte McKenzie and Devansh Patel. We call this the taxing field because nothing will grow here, and that's what the claimed are, a tax on our people. Some say nothing grows because of what happens here with the monsters, that this land is cursed. Others insist it's from radiation even though we've been assured there's no radiation near our village, but if there's no radiation, then why is this field so desolate? I tend to err on the side of science. I mean, once the wars got bad enough, the nukes took out most of the cities, and stray bombs ended up all over the wilds. I was born decades after the wars, but evidence of them is still everywhere. Barren because of radiation or not, the taxing field is the last place anyone wants to end up. Tears stream down my face, and Willow's figure blurs in my vision.

We're opposites like that. Where she burns with anger, I freeze with despair.

Willow and I have always had a bond deeper than anyone could understand. We're two parts to the same whole—like soulmates. But despite the closeness we share, we've suffered through our adolescence with the bitter knowledge that we'd be separated one day. She's to go to the city where the monsters live; I'm to stay here in the village, and that will be the end of *us*.

"Knowing something is going to happen and having it happen are two entirely different things," I whisper to Mama. Having it happen hurts a hell of a lot more. If life isn't cruel enough after the fall of civilization, try being the second half of a twin sister pairing where the first is claimed.

I step forward to go after Willow, but Mama is quick to snatch me back. "This is the way it has to be," she hisses in my ear, voice pleading. This is why Mama and Papa didn't want me to come along today. They knew my emotions would get the better of me. But I had to come. I knew that I'd never be able to accept Willow leaving me unless I saw her go with my own eyes.

I swallow hard, wanting to run anyway, but I stay on our side of the field because Mama is right. If I run after her, they'll kill me. At least, that's what everyone says. I was here once before, last year. Nobody was killed that day, but it certainly felt like it. I wasn't supposed to come, but I did anyway, staying far enough back to avoid notice. I'd watched them take Knox, my boyfriend. Willow had begged me not to fall for him because he had been one of the claimed, and our relationship was doomed from the start, but try telling that to my heart. It didn't listen, and I did fall. Willow had held me for days after that while I mourned his departure. Who will hold me now?

This is the way it has to be. Mama's words echo in my ears. I wish I could silence them, that they weren't the truth.

If Willow and I were identical twins, I'd take her place. Over the years, I've wondered if I'd have the courage to switch lots with her had we been given the genetic opportunity, and now I know the truth. I would. I love Willow more than I love myself. She isn't meant for a life of oppression. Neither am I, for that matter, but this will either break her or kill her. She's *too* strong, and she'll never submit to them, not like I would.

But Willow and I are not identical, so it would be impossible for me to take her place and not have anyone know it. To break the law would mean both our deaths. To give her a chance at survival, I have to let her go. I hate myself for it.

Mama squeezes my hand. She's crying. Papa and little Evan aren't here, but I'm sure wherever they are, they're crying too. They said their goodbyes back at the house because neither could bear to come along for the claiming. I guess some people would rather not witness their worst fears come alive right in front of them.

But I'd rather see the truth—no matter how bad— than spend my life wondering.

Those of us who aren't claimed stand along one end of the field that marks the edge of our village. The unlucky three who must leave during their eighteenth year on the morning of the harvest moon are gathered at the other end. Willow, Charlotte, and Devansh have all prepared for this. The girls have known they were claimed their entire lives since they were given their lot at birth. Devansh could have been spared if his parents had ever birthed a girl, but his mother was blessed with boys only, same as Knox's. So Devansh is the claimed, allowing his family to continue living in our village. Still, being prepared doesn't make this any easier. If Knox was hoping for a little sister to come along and take the burden, he never once showed it publicly, nor privately to me. Devansh doesn't show it either. Some things are simply what they are, and there's no changing it.

My eyes flit from Willow's back, where her long strawberry blonde hair sways side to side over her new green dress, to the tall men barking out orders and lining the claimed up like cattle. These men offer us their protection from the monsters roaming the wilds even though they're also monsters themselves. Monsters and jailers as far as I'm concerned.

Willow's shiny hair is almost pink in this September

morning light, and it catches the eye of one of the men—the leader. He grasps it, running a lock between his greedy fingers, before reaching down to grope her backside. Willow twists from his grip and slaps him across the jaw. The sound echoes across the field like a cracking whip.

Silence.

No.

She didn't just do that.

Mama grips my hand, and our neighbor Mr. Fernsby appears in front of me. He's one of the voyeurs, come to "support us," but I shove him aside, holding my breath and watching helplessly. The man standing in front of Willow shifts into a full-blown wolf. His body transforms with the ripping of clothing as his human flesh deforms into that of an animal. His fur is dark brown, nearly black, and in his wolf form, he's a head taller than my sister. I've never seen the wolf shifters in their wolf bodies, and here one is, standing over Willow, saliva dripping onto her cheek.

Willow doesn't move. She just stands there with her fists clenched tight and her stance wide, as if prepared to battle. "Oh, let them have mercy," Mama whispers. A few of the other men move closer to my sister, but they don't shift into their wolves. They just watch, like me.

The wolf growls, and the guttural sound tears across the field. My insides turn to ice.

"Close your eyes," Mama mutters next to me.

But I don't listen to her. Even though I know what's about to happen, I cannot look away.

He opens his jaws wide, and I will her to run. But Willow's never been a runner. She's a fighter. She's looking straight ahead, even as the razor-sharp teeth come down on her.

The jaws clamp on her head, and I let out a squeak. Mama squeezes my hand again. The wolf lifts Willow into the air, and her body hangs limp, blood gushing from her neck. I should close my eyes now, but I can't. Instead, I watch as he shakes her side to side. Her body flings this way and that until it finally separates into two pieces and goes flying. The wolf drops her head, her pretty pink hair now bright red with blood. Her body lies ten feet away from him.

A scream releases through me, ripping my soul in half. Mama clamps her hand across my mouth. Mr. Fernsby grabs my arms and forces me to turn away. I blink wildly, staring at the dead earth, muffled sobs racking my entire body. My heart aches. I'm weightless and a million pounds all at once. The stench of Willow's coppery blood wafts across the breeze so thick I can almost taste it. I tear away from Mama's hand and fall to my knees, vomiting into the dirt.

This isn't real. This can't be happening.

"Submission," a male voice roars, "subservience, and obedience. Those are the three rules for the claimed."

Three words that all mean the same thing.

I turn on my knees to gaze back over the field, careful to keep my eyes up and away from what's left of Willow. Grief hasn't hit me yet, only shock. But it will.

The man has shifted back from his wolf form. He's naked and is slowly pulling on a pair of pants that one of his underlings has handed him. He's back to being a man, or what appears to be a man. *Father* is a man. *We* are men and women here in our village. Humans. Those wolfish beasts are not men—they're monsters—demons sent to plague us.

"If you want to survive," the wolf shifter continues, addressing the two remaining claimed who stare at him with horrified expressions, "you will follow those rules as if your life depends on it. Because it does." He points to the rest of us across the field. "And so do theirs. Do not forget that your friends and family get to live because of our protection. We could just as easily take all of you as slaves or leave you to the lycans." He smiles sickly as his bronzed skin gleams under the stark light and his shaggy black hair whips in the wind. "But we're far too generous for that."

His companions chuckle.

Hate burns me alive from the inside out. All I want is to destroy him, to kill this disgusting *thing* and every other *thing* like him.

One day, I will.

They're different from the grotesque lycans: they have a pack, they can change at will, they're born *wolf shifters*—not humans infected with a virus that turns them mad at the full moon like the lycanthropes. But to me, they're just as bad as the lycans. Maybe they're even worse.

Things used to be so different before the wars.

Monsters used to hide in the shadows while humans controlled everything, and from the stories, life was good. But then the monsters got tired of hiding—that's when the wars started, and everything changed. There are many whisperings of what happened, of why all of the supernaturals died but shifters didn't, of how lycans came to be, but those are just stories to us now. We don't know what's real and what's not. Maybe too much time has passed, and nobody knows the truth anymore. Or maybe it's like what my father says, that the victors get to choose how history is written.

And that certainly wasn't us humans.

"Now, who are the parents of this defiant little waste of flesh?" The shifter kicks at Willow's slumped body and strolls over to her decapitated head, frowning down on it. "Too bad. She was rather pretty."

My tears have dried under all this fiery hate, and all I can see is red.

Red blood.

Red hate.

Mr. Fernsby shuffles away from where he's been blocking Mama and me. So much for neighborly love and support. Everyone turns to stare at us, their heavy gazes mixed with accusation, fear, and pity.

Mama grips my hand so tightly I might scream. "No," she whispers. "No, no, no, no."

Our village is small—only twenty families—and as long as I have been alive, this has never happened. The firstborn goes to the wolf shifters, and the rest of us work the fields and try to find meaning in our simple lives. I have no idea what happens if a firstborn dies on the day of her claiming.

"Mama, what's going on?"

The wolfman stalks toward us. I can practically hear his heavy feet pounding the dry earth. His bare chest is streaked with blood and dirt, and his muscles ripple with the clenching of his fists.

Mama tightens her grip on my arm. "If the firstborn daughter dies before she is claimed, then the second-born must take her place." Her voice sounds hollow.

A lump forms in my throat, but before I can let a scream loose, the man stands before us, breathing hard. His chest glistens with sweat and the red sheen of my sister's blood. He stares down at my mother. "Your daughter defied me and denied us a claim. What was her name?"

"Willow." Her voice is strong, and I don't know how she could fake that.

His lips thin. "Hmm, pretty name. And who is your second-born?"

"Poppy, my lord." Mama pushes me forward an inch. The wolfman leans down and sniffs my neck. I shiver.

"She smells of age. How is that possible?"

She looks around for a minute, as if willing the others to save us. But nobody says a word. Who would dare?

"Twins, my lord." She closes her eyes for a moment, holding back tears. When she opens them again, she's emotionless, and not one single tear falls. It sends a shiver of warning down my spine.

I look up at the man, hating him even more. An evil smile twists his lips. "How fortunate for us." He shoves his face right in mine, his ice-blue eyes studying me like a map. "Your mother knows how to be respectful to us. Do you?"

I take a small step back and mutter, "Yes."

"Yes, my lord," Mama hisses next to me. Her tone feels like a slap.

The man just stares, and I clear my throat. "Yes, my lord," I say louder than before. My heart is drumming against my ribcage, but from fear or anger or shock, I still don't know.

"Good. Then we won't have to kill two of you today."

He grips my arm, nails sharp as claws, and drags me away from Mama. I cry out and reach for her, but she gives a quick shake of her head. If I want to keep my life and protect what's left of our family, I have to go without a fight. I understand, and I don't even blame her though it feels like a betrayal, but I'm still not prepared for this.

My sister had been attending classes for nearly a year with the other claimed from our village and the villages around us. They were taught how to behave around the wolves, the names of their leaders, and the nuances of shifter culture. I am going in blind. Willow never told me what she learned, and I never asked. It's not that I didn't care. It was just that I didn't want to be reminded that she was leaving me or to think about Knox anymore.

The man dumps me next to Charlotte McKenzie. She's beautiful with her long golden hair braided intricately down her back, her cheeks and lips painted rosy pink, and her virginal white cotton dress perfectly pressed. She and I aren't friends, never have been. She liked Knox, and he liked me, so naturally, she hated me. But she reaches for my hand—I'm no longer her enemy.

Today we are in this together.

CHAPTER 2

THEY MUST REALLY LIKE BLONDES. There are sixteen wolfmen here, ranging in age from older teenagers to adults, and they all stare at Charlotte like she's a juicy meal and they want to be the first to the table. Growing up, her golden hair and rosy complexion made her stand out in our village. She always loved the attention, which was one of the qualities that bothered me most about her. Today, however, her confidence is crumbling under their hunger.

I whisper in her ear. "Do you know what comes next?"

"Silence," the same male who killed Willow barks at me. He's at least fifteen feet away from our walking line. Is his hearing really so good that he could hear my question? Or maybe he just knew I'd spoken. "We will complete the Harvest Moon Ritual by nightfall, and then we'll show you all to your new home."

So he did hear me.

I blink away the tears. It hits me that I'll never see my real home again. I didn't even get to say goodbye. Papa and Evan will be absolutely devastated by the news, and there's nothing I can do to comfort them.

I don't know how long we've been walking. An hour? More? My mind is clearing from the cloud of shock, and all I can think about is everything I've lost.

I open my mouth to ask another question, but Charlotte stops me with the squeeze of her hand and the widening of her eyes. She shakes her head, and images of Willow's decapitation rip through my mind. I can still smell the copper of her blood; I don't know if I'll ever forget it.

I don't speak again.

We walk for what feels like hours, Charlotte and I still gripping each other's hands for stability. The sun rises high in the sky and burns my cheeks, but I can't be bothered to care. My muscles ache. I'm not dressed up like the other women. I'm in brown canvas farming trousers and a button-up shirt used for field work. Our village is harvesting the last of the cotton for the season, and normally, I would be joining the others to work in the fields. In a few weeks, we'd be sitting about in groups and chatting and singing songs while spinning the cotton into fabric. It's hard labor, but it's all I know. What will become of me now?

Eight villages surround the wolf city, and ours is only the second to have been claimed for the day. We're one of the smallest villages, so we have to work extra hard to keep up with the cotton harvest. I don't mind. It's better than this endless walking. We go from village to village, and I always turn away, desperately trying not to listen to the muffled crying as the claimed join our group. By the sixth village, I'm numb inside and out. I'm not holding Charlotte's hand anymore, either. I don't even know when that fell away.

Our walking group has grown. Now there are nineteen of us, fifteen women and four men. Only two more claimings to go——the textile village and the distillery.

Every village has a purpose, from farming to making clothes to raising livestock. Our village grows the cotton and makes the fabric, sending it on to the textile village where they dye it and fashion it into clothing. We share with each other and take care of ourselves despite most of what we produce getting handed over to the wolves. Though, that isn't as bad as losing firstborn daughters or those few oldest sons to them. We do it because the shifters protect us from the lycanthropes who rove the wilds. As bad as the wolf shifters are, at least, they haven't succumbed to a virus that's made the lycans beholden to the moon phases. Lycans will decimate an entire village during one full moon night if given the chance.

It's a steep price to pay but better than losing our entire population in a night. The claiming always takes place during the day of the harvest moon in September. Rumor has it that one time, when I was too young to remember, the textile village had a family who refused to hand over their oldest daughter. As punishment, the shifters did not protect them, and the next day, all but two families in that village had been slaughtered by the lycans.

No one has refused since.

We wait on the outskirts of that textile village now. It's still very small since they lost most of their people years ago, and most of the population is made up of young married couples from the surrounding villages who were trained to make clothes, so they rarely have a child of age to send. I'm a little surprised we stopped, actually. I've been bringing fabric here for years with Papa and don't remember seeing anyone my age.

The men pass around a skein full of water, and we all drink. Charlotte and I haven't left one another's side. More women have joined us like we've all gravitated toward each other, same as lambs do. The men then take out a bag and hand us each an apple, a dry roll, and a chunk of cheese. I guess they don't want us passing out on the way to the city—how thoughtful. I can't help but roll my eyes.

"Do you know their names?" I whisper to Charlotte. We both turn to study our jailers. I hate them all for what they did to Willow, but I'd like to put a name to the one I hate the most, the middle-aged looking one with the bronzed skin and dark hair, who thought he could grope my sister and then kill her for having enough self-respect to slap him.

Charlotte swallows a bite of her apple and locks eyes with him. He nods at her, and she wipes her palms on her dress between bites. "We learned about some of them during our classes. The one in charge is Anders. He's a beta and the alpha's second in command." She jerks her head toward the one who's been paying the most attention to her, his silver eyes never straying from her for long. He's attractive—with dirty blonde hair and a summer tan, and he's younger than the other men here, maybe no older than us. "His name is Grady, and he's also a beta. He's in charge of defense around the villages and is third in command. The rest I don't know."

We finish our meal in silence with the men all still staring at Charlotte's honey blonde hair. That's when they're not staring at the rest of us. I can't stand their attention even if it's fleeting, so I keep my eyes on the dusty ground.

Anders returns a few moments later with a girl who definitely did not dress up for the occasion. She wears a ripped black t-shirt that is so short it doesn't even cover her stomach and denim shorts that are cut off at mid-thigh. Her dark hair is cut severely short, and it looks like it's been hacked off with a kitchen knife. Charlotte sucks in a breath, and I know what she's thinking. While the claimed men have to razor their hair as short as possible, the claimed women aren't allowed to cut their hair shorter than the bottom of their shoulder blades.

This girl must've cut hers last night. I'm surprised she's still alive.

I like her already.

Anders shoves her in line right in front of me. I glance at the rest of the men and see that Grady's expression has changed from a persistent scowl to one of utter shock. Anders brings his hand to a section of the girl's hair and gives a hard yank. "You'll pay for this in the city. If we hadn't already lost one today, you'd be dead."

"Better dead than a slave to you." Then, she spits in his face. Anders is not having a good day. No one moves for a moment. Fur ripples across Anders's arms, and before I know what's happening, Grady is there, shoving Anders hard in the chest.

Anders growls. A flash of a wolf face comes and then goes.

"She's mine," Grady yells. "No one touches her." He crosses his arms and glares at the rest of the wolfmen.

"I belong to no man." The girl scowls at Grady. "Especially not an animal like you."

But Anders immediately relaxes and ignores the girl. Then, he guffaws, and I'm completely stunned. I thought for sure I was going to see a repeat of Willow's death. Why had no one stood up for Willow, but this girl is still alive? Guilt barbs deep because it should've been me who helped my sister. Anders doubles over in laughter, but no one else seems to understand the humor. He pulls himself together and places a hand on Grady's shoulder. Grady hasn't moved from his spot. "You have fun with that one." He walks back up to the front of the line. "Moving out," he calls.

Grady grips the girl by the upper arm and drags her out of the line despite her kicking at him. He eventually picks her up and carries her on his back like she weighs nothing. I have no idea what just happened, and I want to ask Charlotte, but I know I'll get into trouble if I do. Somehow, I don't think any of these men will care to save me. I'm not uniquely beautiful like Charlotte, nor am I dressed to enhance my femininity like so many here. I don't have a resilient spirit like the girl Grady has taken a liking to, and there's nothing about me that shines as she does. I was never supposed to be claimed, and maybe that makes me less worthy than the others. But why should I care? None of this is right, anyway.

My feet are achy, and my head is heavy as we head to the last village, the distillery. It's the only village that we don't have a lot of regular connections with. It's the largest in the area—fifty families. They have the most wealth and nearly all the amenities that the wolf city is rumored to have. Papa always told me to never go near the distillery boys when they came to our village to trade goods. The boys from other villages would attend our dances so the young people could court, but I was never allowed to dance with the ones from this place. And when we arrive in the village square where they apparently do their claiming, I think I understand why.

Their girls are nothing like our girls.

There are six of them. It's a lot. They're not dressed in long cotton dresses like the rest of us—or, in my case, ugly trousers. These women are proudly showing off their skin with short and tight outfits that I've never seen the likes of before. Some appear to be made of leather and others the sheerest cotton that leaves nothing to the imagination. How did they even get such clothes? I blush and look away. Every girl at this claiming proudly displays her cleavage and has painted her face with more rouge and charcoal than I've ever seen on a single person.

And none of them are crying. Not one.

In fact, their expressions are smug, like going to the wolf city is the best thing that's ever going to happen to them. But the two claimed men from this village look just as dejected as the rest of us, with their downcast eyes and slumped shoulders.

What do the women of the distillery know that I don't?

CHAPTER 3

WE ROUND A BEND, and the wolf city appears on the horizon. I'm a bit underwhelmed. Not that I was looking forward to it or anything, but the way Papa described the cities, I always thought they would have large, looming buildings. This one doesn't. It's shoved full of buildings, but aside from a few spires, they all appear short and squat.

We stop at the edge of the river. There is a large bridge, but it's got a gaping hole right in the middle of it. I wonder how we are going to manage to cross it safely. An image of myself falling through crumbling concrete and into the rushing water flashes through my mind, and I forget to breathe. Fortunately, we sit down in the tall grass to rest. The humidity wraps itself around me like a wet blanket, and I wipe the sweat from my forehead.

Grady passes around the skein of water once again, and Anders disappears down the embankment.

I count the number of the claimed to distract myself from the unknown. I have no idea what's coming, and I don't want to think about it. There are twenty-eight total now, twenty-two women and six young men. Twenty-eight people who have friends and family back home, who had full lives before the claiming changed everything.

The women from the distillery village are all flirting with the wolfmen. They're laughing and touching them on the arms, acting in a way that the people of my village would find scandalous. I shiver and look away. I will never willingly touch one of these men. They are monsters. *This* is monstrous.

Anders returns. His black wavy hair hangs over one eye, and when he brushes it away, I notice a lot of the girls are watching him. He's older than most of the wolves and has at least ten years on us, probably more. There's an experienced edge to him that these women seem to find appealing. But what if I told them about what he did to Willow? Would they still look at him like a prize, or would they see him as a curse, as I do?

"The boats have arrived," he calls out. "The claimed men will follow Grady, and the women will follow me."

Devansh Patel stands as if to be first to the boat, but then he makes a run for it, heading straight toward the river. He jumps in, splashing water in an arc as he swims wildly, almost like he's trying to rescue a drowning man. Maybe he is—but it's not someone else's life he's after saving; it's his own. Where he thinks he's going, I have no clue. My heart aches as I picture his family back home. What will happen to them now that he's run from his obligation? Charlotte and I exchange worried glances.

Anders laughs. "He does realize it's a full moon tonight, right?"

Grady shrugs. "I guess he'd rather drown or be killed by lycans than be claimed by us." Then, Grady sighs, annoyed, and flashes his eyes toward the textile village woman he was carrying earlier. "Don't even think about trying the same thing."

She folds her arms over her chest and glares right back.

Grady points to one of his men. "Take care of this, please." The man tugs off his clothing and shifts into a massive gray wolf. He paws at the ground, snarls loudly, and then darts to the river's edge. He runs along the bank, faster than the water itself, until disappearing into the horizon.

I don't know how Devansh is going to die, but I'm certain his death is imminent. I look away to the boats bobbing against the shore and will my mind to think of something else. He wasn't necessarily a friend, but we still lived parallel lives. That said, I can't handle his death along with my sister's. I just can't. As selfish as it is, I force the Patel family from my mind.

"Let's go," Anders calls out to us women, and we don't dally.

Papa has a small rowboat that he sometimes takes out to catch fish on the river. I've gone with him a few times, but I get sick on boats. Willow went with him more often. She loved the water. Mama called her a fish and me a bird. Now, Willow's dead, and I'm being escorted to a cage, but at least I'm alive. My heart tightens to think of her like she was on those days we went to the river. I still can't believe that she's gone.

These boats are much larger than Papa's rowboat, and we all fit on one of them easily. A young man stands at the rear of the boat. He's way too scrawny to be a wolf. He must be one of the claimed slaves. If this is what's in store for me, I can handle this. It wouldn't be a life I choose, but I could drive a boat. It might even be more fun than growing cotton.

I let out a sigh of relief. I've been imagining all the horrors the wolf shifters could do to me, but now I realize that the claimed probably just become their servants. It wouldn't be any harder than the work we do in the cotton fields. Either way, they own us. The worst thing on this side is that I'll never get to see my family again.

A roaring sounds from the back of the boat, and we shoot off faster than I thought was possible. I cover my ears, and Charlotte laughs. "What's that noise?" I ask, speaking louder than I have all day.

"It's an engine. The cities have more technology than we do. We were taught about it, but seeing it is entirely different."

We both gape in awe as we fly down the river. We bounce on the waves, and I hold on to Charlotte's arm, certain we're all going to be flung off this thing. The sun is setting, painting the sky orange, and the city up ahead is lit with strange colored unnatural lights. The houses perch on the river, all squished together and painted bright colors. Men hang off of balconies and hoot as we pass.

If I weren't here under these circumstances, I might enjoy myself. The other girls are. One of the distillery girls has an arm looped through Anders's, and she's pointing to things on the shore while he's speaking animatedly to her. He turns his head and catches my eye. I hold his gaze, hoping he can see the hatred in my stare. He killed my sister, and someday he will pay. As if reading my thoughts and finding them entertaining, his lips curl up into a sadistic smile, and he winks.

Charlotte unhitches my arm from hers and scoots away.

Anders laughs and breaks our gaze. He slows the boat, pulling up to a dock. It's painted with a bright turquoise paint that's peeling along the edges. We climb out and line up on the shore. I'm the only girl in work pants, but maybe that's not such a bad thing. Maybe they'll give me a job that will keep me busy. I don't mind hard work. Plus, I'll need to stay busy if I'm going to survive the grief of losing my family, not to mention the entire future I had planned for myself.

Anders waves his hand at someone approaching us. My breath catches. Dread and longing swirl in my chest. I'm frozen, staring. He's the tallest young man I've ever seen, at least six-foot-five, with broad shoulders and a commanding stance. But it's not his height that stops me. It's his beauty. He is without question the most stunning boy I've ever seen, with a sculpted athletic build, piercing blue eyes, honey bronzed skin, and jet-black hair that curls down around his shoulders. As he walks past, the other wolfmen bow to him. Next to me, the girls stand taller.

"Say hello to the alpha," Anders says before bowing along with the others. "This is Prince Ryne Tremaine."

We're a chorus of breathy hellos, and I'm suddenly wishing I were dressed like the other girls or had Charlotte's blonde hair or just something, *anything,* to make me stand out. I mentally pinch myself. What is going on with me? I should hate him—I do hate him. If it weren't for his men, Willow would still be alive. If he's the alpha, then maybe that's the explanation for why I find him so attractive, for why I want him to notice me so much— surely an alpha is born with a natural presence. But it doesn't matter because Mama always said it's what's on the inside that counts, and I can guarantee that whatever is inside this creature is rotten. I need to stay far, far away from him.

His eyes survey us, unreadable, until they catch on mine and grow curious, then hateful, and then . . . He turns on his heel and storms away.

Anders chuckles. "Sorry, ladies, he must not like the looks of this year's claimed." His eyes roam over us and lock with mine. My chest burns. I don't know when, and I don't know how, but he will pay for what he did to Willow. A slow, creepy grin slides over his lips, and he winks at me. "I do though. Perhaps I'll choose my mate from one of you." His eyes never leave mine. Titters come from the distillery girls, and I break his gaze. All of the girls are glaring at me like I killed their cat. I drop my eyes to stare at my scuffed boots.

"What's he talking about?" I hiss to Charlotte.

"I have no idea," she whispers back.

A vehicle pulls up with a long flatbed trailer behind it. "Up you go," Anders says, and the men corral us up on the trailer. I wish I had some clue as to what was going on, but nothing makes sense. At least we don't have to walk anymore. Anders and his men sit on the edges of the trailer, and all of us girls congregate in the middle.

The distillery girls fluff each other's hair and yank down their shirts so even more of their cleavage shows. One tries to sit next to Anders, but he shoos her back to the rest of us. The ride is rough, and Charlotte and I cling together so we don't tumble over. Darkness has fallen, but lights line the street. A few men walk along the edges of the road, but it's mostly empty.

Up ahead I see more lights and crowds. There are far more people here than in my village. More bodies in a single spot than I could've ever imagined. Charlotte grips my hand tightly. She's been hot and cold with me all day, but I don't mind. At least I'm not the only one who doesn't know what's going on. We turn a corner and are met with music blaring and lights strobing. I've never seen anything like it. I wonder at the bright lights but have to cover my ears to the unnaturally loud thumping music. The truck drives slowly down the street so everyone can get a good look at us. The sidewalks are full of extremely tall, muscular men, most of whom are shirtless. They howl as we pass. I suck in a breath and catch the scent of alcohol and sweat.

Something is very wrong here.

The distillery girls all start dancing and blowing kisses, lapping up the attention. The rest of us huddle closer together, uncomfortable and afraid. A man lunges for the trailer, but Anders jumps off the side and shoves him back. "The claimed aren't for your taking. Not yet anyway."

The man growls and steps back, but his eyes linger on us, and a hungry smirk crosses his scarred face.

"What does he mean by that?" I ask Charlotte again,

but I think I might know. I also think I might be sick.

My initial impression of just being servants might not be correct, and I'm nervous because these men are acting like they want our bodies. Knox and I had kissed plenty, so I have a general idea of what it means for a man and woman to be together, but I can't imagine being with one of *them*. Is that what we are?

Whores?

That's what my mother called girls who didn't have husbands and would spend their nights with different men. I'd never met one, but Mama warned me about becoming one. Especially when she saw how much time I'd been spending with Knox. "Poppy," she'd said. "That boy is claimed and will never be able to be your husband. Don't go whoring yourself out to him." Then I made the mistake of asking what whoring meant.

I never asked Mama a question about it again. Now, seeing what I might have to do, I wish I had. I can't help but wonder what Willow would think of all of this. No doubt she'd tell the distillery girls off for their behavior and challenge the wolves for engaging in whatever this is. No doubt she'd be the center of attention through it all, even more so than Charlotte. Her strawberry hair and fiery personality always made the boys crazy.

We continue down the bumpy road, coming to a halt in front of a large stage.

"Follow me," Anders calls to us, "and be careful not to get bit."

CHAPTER 4

"HE'S JOKING, RIGHT?" I squeak and reach for Charlotte again. This time, she rolls her eyes at me and peels herself out of my grip, rushing ahead to walk with the distillery girls. I know we weren't friends back home, but it wasn't like we were enemies either. Her rejection stings.

"Probably not joking." The girl from the textile village hooks her arm through mine. "Will you getta look at these sickos?" She grimaces at the leering men. They're all ages, from young teens to adults, and they're acting like we're the only women they've ever seen, but that can't be true.

I swallow hard. "I don't understand."

She turns with a pitying look, honey-colored eyes creasing at the corners. "What village are you from? You never heard the rumors?"

"We help grow and harvest the cotton," I say. "Northwest."

"Ah . . ." She frowns. "Well, in Southeast, let's just say we're close enough to East to see and hear a lot of things that go on between them and the wolves."

East is the official name for the distillery village. The eight villages go by the geographic location to the city, either that or what they're known for making. I always assumed we all led similar lives and only interacted with the wolves for the claiming, beyond them protecting the borders, of course.

"What goes on?" I ask, but I'm interrupted by Anders ushering us onto one side of the stage. I look away from the crowds and up into the sky.

The harvest moon hangs low above the buildings. It appears closer than I ever remember, the orange glow mesmerizing. If I were where I was supposed to be, I'd be sitting outside our modest home with my family and neighbors, missing Willow and wishing her the best. Papa would've built a fire to keep us warm while we exchange stories with our friends, who'd be trying to cheer us up after the claiming.

I look away. I can't be bothered with the moon tonight. I'll never look at it the same way again.

Anders raises his hands and howls—actually howls. The crowd of men follows suit. It's so deafening I have to cover my ears again. The alpha strides onto the stage, and my eyes lock on his face. He's smiling, and it feels like the first time I've ever seen a boy smile. Ryne, his name is Ryne—it dances around my head like lightning bugs in summertime. But then I remember what he is, and I can hardly think of him as a boy, let alone as someone I should be attracted to.

"Welcome to the harvest!" he bellows over the crowd. Their howls transform to cheers. The buzz of anticipation is so intense I can hardly breathe.

The textile girl tightens her grip on my arm and ignores the crowd. "I'm Joanna, by the way. What's your name?"

"Poppy."

The howling stops, and everything goes silent. I can practically hear my heart thundering in my chest. I wonder...can the monsters hear it too?

"The harvest is always a favorite time of year for the pack," the alpha continues. "Are you ready to see who your new girls will be?"

Another howl from the men, and I swallow. I don't like the looks of this at all. I drop my eyes so I don't have to see the crowd. We're hidden on the back of the stage, but I have a feeling we'll be thrust front and center before too long. What comes after that is anyone's guess.

"Ladies," he calls, and I jerk my head back up. He's not pointing at us. He's waving a group of girls over from the other side of the stage.

They are dressed quite differently from us. Each wears a shimmering ball gown that is cut extra low in the chest to reveal their figures. The dresses are made from beautiful fabrics I've never seen before, certainly nothing that can be found in Northwest. These come in a rainbow of colors, and they flare out at the knees. The fabric trails each of them, actually dragging along the stage. Mother would be shocked at the wastefulness. There are nine women in total, and with the exception of different colored hair, they all look so similar from where I'm standing.

They stop near the front of their stage, shoulders arched gracefully. I can't see their faces, so I don't know if they are smiling.

"Four of my betas have chosen to retire this year. Come and choose your mates," the alpha says.

It's then that I notice a large group of muscled men. Some are standing on the far end of the stage, and some are down in the crowd. Anders and Grady stand with the ones on the stage. They've cleaned up and are now wearing black pants and jackets with white shirts underneath. There are so many men that they blend together in a sea of black and white.

But there are four who stand apart from the rest, four who stare at the women as if they're about to enjoy a long-awaited feast. My stomach hardens.

"Who are they?" I hiss to Joanna.

She snorts. "Don't you know anything? Those are the betas. Some of those men hope to make us their wives, though we're all going to end up as babymakers—

that's for sure." I just gape at her, and she rolls her eyes, continuing on. "Listen up, there are one hundred betas in all. When they retire from leading lower ranked wolves, they take on an advisory role and get to choose a wife."

"Babymakers?" I'm still caught on that word.

"Yep. But trust me, it's better for us to be married off to a beta than not being chosen at all." She looks out to the other men in the crowd, the ones who aren't dressed up, and scowls.

"Make your selections," the alpha bellows.

Four of the men each choose a girl by pulling her into his arms and kissing her deeply. The crowd loves it. When the couples are finished, the men take their mates and disappear. Five girls are left. One of them falls to her knees and breaks out in sobs. An older woman rushes forward, peeling the crying girl off the floor. I catch a look at her face and gasp. I know her. She's Julia, a girl from my village. She went through the claiming last year when Knox was taken. Our eyes meet, and she screams out, "Get away while you still can, Poppy!"

That does it. Anders is there in an instant, striking her down. Blood arcs across the stage. She sobs even harder, her mouth now dripping with blood, as the older woman ushers her and the other girls away.

"They will be at the mating houses by midnight." The alpha continues speaking to the crowd as if all this is completely normal. "And you lot won't have to wait any longer."

More howls.

Bile rises in my throat, and my stomach clenches. I'm horrified by what is happening even though I don't fully understand what it is. A blinding spotlight shines on us, and I flinch.

The alpha waves his hand toward us. "I'm pleased to introduce the new crop from this year. We've had our most fruitful season yet. Wouldn't you agree?"

Ryne just called us crops, and now I definitely don't like him. I glare his way as we're pushed out onto the center of the stage. He doesn't even notice.

"Betas, who wants to claim their bride from this group?"

The distillery girls smile and wave at the remaining men in suits. Charlotte is now among them. She's pulled her dress down lower too. Joanna snorts. "Fools."

Grady steps forward immediately and gives Joanna a hearty smile and a wink.

"I think he likes you," I whisper.

"He said we're fated, but he's delusional. I'm going to escape before he can get his hands on me."

"Escape?"

"Yep. You wanna come with?"

Hope burns in my heart, but the image of Willow's head flashes through my mind. I have no idea what running away would look like or what would come of it.

Tears sting my eyes even to imagine the idea. "I don't know," I whisper back. What would that mean for my family? And how would we even make it out of here alive, let alone survive the wilds?

Anders steps forward, his eyes heavy on me, and I shiver. I could never be with him. If that is my fate, then I will run away with Joanna, fate be damned.

Three more men step forward who were not on the journey to retrieve us.

"Five. Not bad. And we have twenty-two claimed, so don't worry, men. You'll have fresh meat soon. The Wolf Moon Festival isn't far off."

Another howl from the alpha sends the rest of the crowd into a frenzy. The sound is deafening, but something instinctual tells me not to cover my ears or let my fear show. I don't flaunt it like some of the other girls, but I stand a little taller and shoot the alpha a scowling glance.

He's looking back at me, not so angry this time, but maybe a little intrigued. He sees my expression and smiles. Part of me wants to rip that smile right off his face, and the other part can't help but wonder how he became the alpha—the other part wants to know his whole story. He looks younger than most of the betas. And he's strong and big, but he doesn't have that razor edge that Anders has, nor the cruel energy that lives among his pack.

"He's the sickest one here, you know?" Joanna hisses low. "You'd be smart to stay away from him."

"You're right. I will." My voice cracks. I want to believe her, but for some inexplicable reason, I don't.

As if he heard us, he chuckles darkly and nods once toward Joanna.

Something guttural screeches above us. I peer up at the buildings just as a flash of gray catapults from a nearby roof and onto the stage. The creature's eyes are bloodshot. Its mouth rears open to reveal teeth as long as fingers. His form hulks twice as large as anyone here as he extends up onto his hind legs.

"Lycan!" Charlotte cries seconds before it lunges toward the alpha.

CHAPTER 5

THE ALPHA DODGES his attacker and immediately transforms into his wolf form, letting his clothing fall in torn strips on the stage. His wolf self is nearly as tall as his human self, with sleek black fur and glowing eyes the same bright blue. He growls at the lycan—a sound so dark and haunting that I'm certain I'll remember it forever. All of the men follow their alpha and shift into their wolves. Good thing too because three more lycans crash onto the stage. The last is the biggest, and the impact sends splinters of wood flying in all directions.

All the girls scream and huddle together as the battle erupts around us.

The lycans stand on hind legs and swipe their claws and teeth at the wolves. The wolves are large animals, but the lycans are something else. They're a mutation—half-human, half-wolf—and entirely grotesque. The wolves may be smaller, but they're faster and organized. They move together in quick formations, almost as if they can communicate telepathically. Perhaps they can.

I find myself on the outside of the circle of girls along with Joanna and Charlotte. Most of the distillery girls are in the middle. Many are already crying. Joanna grabs my hand. "We should run away," she hisses in my ear.

"Are you crazy? They'll kill us."

"This might be our only shot."

I shake my head. She might be right, but there was no way on earth that I was about to run away with lycans on the loose. I've always called the shifters the monsters, but the truth is staring me right in the face now. The lycanthropes are the ones who come in the middle of the night and kill humans like it's a sport, so they're the true monsters. I'll take my chances with the wolf shifters.

Joanna breaks away from us, and immediately, a lycan leaps after her. He's twice her height with dark gray fur and wicked-looking claws. He lunges, but before he can grab her, a light golden-brown wolf leaps in between them, throwing the creature off balance.

Joanna stumbles back to my side, gripping my hand as the wolf and lycan fight right in front of us. The lycan slashes at the wolf, but he's too fast. The lycan changes tactics and lunges for our group, exposing his side, and the wolf sinks his teeth into its throat, tearing the flesh away. The lycan drops to the ground, and the brown wolf positions himself right in front of Joanna.

I'd bet my life that he is Grady, but I don't tell Joanna that.

"Are you okay?" I ask her.

She nods even though she has a death grip on my hand. The entire stage is shaking with the fight. Down on the ground, wolves snarl and slash at the remaining lycans. I question whether I'm going to make it out of here alive tonight, and that makes me press farther back into the group of girls. Everywhere I look, there are claws and teeth and blood. Even the crisp air smells of copper.

The stage rumbles beneath my feet, and I bring my gaze up to watch the biggest lycan break away from his fight with the alpha and charge straight for us. He jumps high and lands right on top of our group, knocking us to our backs. Girls scream, but I don't. A stillness settles over my mind, and I decide I'm *not* going to die today. I push at the rough fur, unsure of what part of his body is over me. Joanna and I break away by crawling on our hands and knees. Blood soaks into my pants, and for a second I worry that it's mine, but I don't think it is. The light brown wolf appears right next to us, his muzzle nudging Joanna along. She swats at him, but he doesn't let up. I expect him to turn back and go after the lycan, but he stays with Joanna.

A streak of black rushes toward the lycan, but before the alpha can reach him, the monster grabs one of the claimed girls and takes off with her. A smaller lycan disengages from his fight and grabs another girl who's cowering near the edge of the stage. She lets out a shrill scream, and then she's being dragged away as well. The wolves howl, and I have to cover my ears. Most of them take off after the two lycans who grabbed the girls, but the light brown wolf still stays by Joanna's side.

Silence descends on us. Compared to the cacophony from before, it's quiet enough to hear a pin drop.

No one is fighting anymore. People are bloodied and bruised. I'm certain a few of the wolves have died, but everyone on stage seems alive.

Joanna's wolf shifts back into his human form, and of course, it's Grady. I avert my eyes. He's naked.

"What the hell were you thinking?" he growls at Joanna.

She crosses her arms and smirks at him. She seems unabashed by his naked body, but several other girls stare or look away with reddened faces. "That I didn't want to be killed by a lycan. I thought I'd take my chances away from where they were fighting."

A young man brings Grady a pair of pants, and he jerks them on. "You're lucky I was here, or you'd be dead. Or worse, turned into one of them." He hovers over her, his nostrils flared. Joanna never breaks eye contact. She doesn't thank him or cower. If he's a beta and used to being in charge of a couple hundred underlings, then perhaps he's met his match in someone as stubborn and confident as Joanna.

Prince Ryne jogs over wearing simple pants that hang low on his hips. The muscles of his chest ripple under the smears of blood, dirt, and sweat. I can't seem to tear my eyes away from him. *This* is his element— war, pain, protection. What does that say about me, to be so attracted to him right now? But part of me hates him, so I try to cling to that part.

"Were any of you bitten?" It's the first question out of his mouth. I think I know why.

The boy who handed Grady his pants raises a shaky hand.

Ryne hangs his head low. "I'm so sorry, pup."

"What does that mean?" one of the girls whispers. But we all knew that a single bite from a lycan would turn you into one of them. I don't know what it will do to a shifter.

"Nobody else was bitten?" he asks. We shake our heads no. "Good. A lycan bite will turn a human," he confirms, "but it will kill a wolf. Either way, the outcome is . . . gruesome." He flinches on the last word. Emotional, not because he's afraid but because he's regretful. I'm completely mesmerized by him and once again disgusted with myself for it. Why does this keep happening to me? Remember, this man keeps traditions that caused Willow's death. He's enabled rituals that have caused us claimed girls to be standing here tonight under the full moon instead of safe at home with our families.

I knew the wolves hated the lycans as much as we did, if not more so, and now I understand why. Wolves are nearly invincible and live long lives, but if a lycan bite can kill them, then perhaps they're almost as vulnerable as humans. The wolves are mostly back in their human form now, and they seem shaken. They aren't nearly as confident as they had been before the lycans attacked.

The young boy kneels before his alpha. "Please, Prince Ryne, have mercy."

Grady hands Ryne a long, silver sword. The glint of it flashes orange under the moonlight. I've heard silver can kill the lycans, but what is he going to do with it to this young shifter? Clearly, the pup is no lycan.

He answers my question with the swing of his arm, the sword arcing toward the boy to sever his head from his body. It rolls to stop at my feet.

I scream. I scream in terror, but mostly, it's anger that shreds my throat. "How is that merciful?" I can't help the accusation bursting from my lips as I try to ignore the decapitated head. "How can you do such a thing to a child?"

Ryne strides forward and catches my face in his hands. His fingers are coated in blood, and his grip is tight, fingertips pressing into my cheeks. He's inches from my face, those blue eyes peering right down into the very depths of my soul. "That pup would've died an excruciating death akin to lethal poisoning. The lycan venom would have cooked him from the inside out and taken days to slowly eat away at his body and sanity. Now, tell me again that I wasn't merciful?"

I can't breathe. I can't blink. I can't move.

Charlotte elbows me, and I snap out of my defiance, nodding against his fingers. "No, my lord. You gave him a painless death."

"That's what I thought." He releases me and steps back, surveying the lot of us. I immediately miss his hands on my face, and it's all I can do to not reach out for him. Again, this must be some kind of draw to him being the alpha. Surely, even humans can't help but react to pack hierarchy when it's so strong like this. I quickly glance around, and the rest of the girls seem just as enthralled by Ryne as I am.

So that's it. I force myself to go back to hating the man.

There were twenty-two claimed females, and now there are twenty. The two taken by the lycans are likely already dead.

"I apologize about tonight, ladies." The alpha straightens, and his expression relaxes. "The lycans don't often make it past our guards, but sometimes accidents happen. They've managed to attack your villages in the past, have they not?"

We nod our agreement. It happens. I'm pretty sure it happens anyway, though a lycan attack hasn't been seen in my village since I've been alive. Our wolf shifter guards do their job well, or maybe our village is small enough that the lycans want a bigger target.

"You'd be wise to be alert during every full moon." He looks around at the aftermath of the battle, runs a hand through his long, disheveled hair, and then sighs. "Welcome to the Carolina Wolf Pack. You're one of us now."

CHAPTER 6

RYNE WAVES ANDERS OVER. "Get them to the house as quickly as possible. Be on the lookout for any rogue lycans. We've already lost two girls tonight. I don't want to lose any more."

Anders gives a nod. "What about the dead?"

"I'll have the other betas gather them. We'll burn the bodies in the morning."

Anders heads for us. I scoot closer into the middle of the girls and find Joanna's hand. She stiffens at first but then squeezes mine back. I'm used to being close to another female because of Willow, and now that she's gone, I can't help but seek Joanna out. Grady still stands on her other side and watches her like she's made of porcelain. I don't know why he's determined to protect her, but I know that if I stay close by her side, I will be safer by association. Charlotte comes up along my other side. Her shirt is soaked with blood.

"What happened to you?" I ask.

She gapes at me. "The same thing that happened to you." She points down.

My trousers and shoes are splattered with blood as well. "Ugh, that will never come out."

Charlotte loops her arm through mine. "It doesn't matter. They will give us all new clothes anyway."

She's been so fickle with me today, but I don't have the energy to care.

"How do you know that?" Clothing takes a lot of time and work. We're supplied with it in exchange for growing the cotton and turning it into fabric, but even then, we only get three new outfits a year.

"We were to bring nothing with us but the clothes on our back." She rolls her eyes. "They told us at the claiming meetings."

Well, I wasn't at the claiming meetings, and Charlotte knows exactly why. Maybe she's not really interested in being my friend, or maybe she's not thinking and wouldn't deliberately try to hurt my feelings. I decide to give her the benefit of the doubt and let it go.

We shuffle off the stage and back to the trailer we rode on. Will I be considered ignorant because I did not attend any of the meetings? I know nothing that I'm supposed to. I should've been a better sister and talked to Willow about what went on in those meetings. I know she'd have told me everything I wanted to know, even if she wasn't supposed to. We never kept secrets. My heart aches to know she died with all of my secrets hidden away inside her. So many are lost now—years and years of memories—just gone.

The trailer rumbles down the cobblestone streets. The sidewalks are empty now, and I stare at the houses as we pass. They are all different colors, three or four stories high, long and narrow. Most have lights on in the windows, but the curtains are drawn. I still can't believe they can light up like that. I've heard of electricity, but we don't have it back home. I feel like I've stepped into an entirely different world.

I wonder which house will become ours and if we will stay together. I may not know Joanna very well, but I like her better than any of the other girls, and maybe next time there's a chance, I'll have the courage to run off with her. Even as I think it, I worry I'm not brave enough. That was always Willow's job.

The trailer stops near the water, away from all the houses, and I spot the boat from before. I groan. "Not another boat ride."

"It's the fastest and safest way," Grady replies. "Don't worry. You'll get used to them." For the first time, I wonder what Grady's underling did with Devansh Patel, assuming they caught him. Maybe Devansh got away and won't have to be a claimed boy after all. Knox's pretty face pops into my mind, and I push it back down into the mental box I've used to lock away that particular heartbreak.

We all scramble onto the boat; it roars to life and flies up the river this time. The moon is so high in the sky, so bright that I can hardly see the stars. It casts yellow light on the many houses and buildings along the river, but as we get farther away from the city, the houses get farther and farther apart. I can't help but keep a look out for lycans. What if there are more out there, hunting us right now? I tuck my arms tight against my body and try not to shiver.

We come around a corner, and I spot a massive, brick plantation home. There are a couple of these back in the village, but nobody lives in them. They're used for meeting spaces. I've always wondered what it must have been like years ago when they were used as homes. I never thought I would get to live in one myself, and given the circumstances, I wish I wasn't about to find out.

Smoke curls out of its many chimneys, and soft light glows from every window. The boat slows and heads for the dock near the house. A rusted sign with moss growing along the edge has words written across it, but I can't read it.

"Drayton Hall," Joanna says in a whisper.

Charlotte turns on her with a little gasp, "You can read?"

Joanna sighs. "I guess mine is one of the only villages

left that still cares about education, but I suppose I shouldn't be surprised."

Charlotte huffs and glares at her. "We've never had anyone who could read to even teach us, so get off your high horse." She gives me a little look like she wants me to get mad at Joanna too, but I hold my hands up. I'm not getting between these two.

"Typical." Charlotte pushes past me to join the distillery girls. That just may have been my last chance to befriend her. But honestly, if it wasn't going to happen during the eighteen years we lived in the same village, it wasn't likely to happen today just because we've been thrown into a traumatizing situation together. I smile at Joanna and hope she doesn't ditch me. I've never *not* had someone.

"This place." Joanna nods to the house and whispers, "it has a dark history. Do you believe in ghosts?"

I roll my eyes. "No. Do you?"

"No, but if I did, I'd definitely think this place was haunted. Do you know about what the humans used to do here hundreds of years ago?"

I shake my head.

"They kept slaves," she whispers.

A haunting chill creeps through my awareness as Anders leads us to the front of the three-story square house. It's a dark red brick with four gleaming white columns up the front. Two identical staircases lead up to the front porch, and we climb them without slowing.

Anders knocks on the door while we stand huddled together on the checkered flooring. I stare at my work boots. The tips are covered in mud and blood and will surely make a mess in a place like this. The massive home is made from different materials than I'm used to back home. Out in our village, we live in little three-room houses. We don't have running water or electricity. We do our cooking over fires, not that we have a lot of meat. It's mostly boiling vegetables. We get our water from a well. We trade with the villages for bread and other necessities. Living in Northwest, we never had anything like this. Life was simple, but at least we were safe.

The door opens, and I immediately recognize the woman standing in the doorway as the same one who had escorted last year's girls onto the stage before us earlier tonight.

"Hello, ladies!" She beams at us as if our horrible night hadn't even happened. "Please, come in! It's getting cold out there."

We shuffle into the entry room. Same as outside, this room has two intricately carved staircases on either side that lead up to the higher levels. The floor in here is polished wood and gleaming without a speck of dirt. The walls are painted a soft greenish-blue, and the ceiling is white with carved detailing unlike anything I've seen. It's stunning.

"You must be exhausted." She claps her hands,

and a couple of other older women appear. "Please take the claimed to their sleeping quarters," she tells them and then levels us with a knowing look. "You've had a big day. It's going to be hard, but please do try to get some rest. Tomorrow, we start your training."

"Training for what?" Joanna juts out her hip in challenge.

Grady chuckles low. Her insolence only seems to make him like her even more. I'll admit I like it too. It makes me feel stronger to be next to her.

The woman isn't fazed one bit by Joanna's outburst. "What's your name, dear?"

"Joanna." The girl is fearless.

"Ah, our one claimed from the textile village of Southeast. It's nice to meet you." Joanna says nothing, and the woman continues. "Well, Joanna, what do you think the word claimed means?"

"That the patriarchal wolf society has enslaved women into forced breeding."

The room falls into a hushed silence. I don't know what that word means, patriarchal, but from Joanna's tone, it can't be good.

Anders rushes forward, his arm outstretched to strike Joanna down, but Grady pummels him to the ground. We scream and scatter out of the way. Not Joanna though. She doesn't move a muscle. "Well," she huffs. "Am I wrong?"

The older woman does the opposite of what I expect. She smiles. "You're not wrong."

Anders growls, shifting right there in the middle of the crowded room. I press my back against the wall. The older woman throws open the door and yells, "Get out! There is no shifting allowed in this house."

Anders snarls at her but leaves. Grady stands, wiping blood from his chin and leveling Joanna with a look. "I won't always be here to protect you, mate."

She glowers. "I'm not your mate. Now leave, and join the rest of your dogs!"

The energy is so intense I can practically taste it. Grady shakes his head, chuckling again, and leaves.

The older woman tuts heavily and brushes her hands along her skirt like this is all normal in her world. Maybe it is. "You can call me Madame Delphine. I was planning to discuss this tomorrow, but Joanna is correct. You are here to mate with the wolves."

My mind races to put all the puzzle pieces together. I should've known—there were so many clues—but the shock still hits me hard. "Why?" I squeak out.

The distillery girls laugh.

Delphine catches my gaze and holds it. "What's your name, honey?"

I can't tell if she's normally this warm or if this is a trick. "Poppy."

"Well, Poppy, have you noticed any female wolf shifters since arriving in the city?"

My mind combs through the events of the day. "No."

"That's because the wolf shifter genes predominantly produce male offspring. Only one in a hundred shifter children are born female. That's a problem for them, don't you think?"

I nod, my face growing hot.

"And so, you, Poppy—and all of you—are here to be the solution. The sooner you accept that, the better."

"And if we don't accept it?" Joanna snaps, her eyes narrowed in challenge.

"Then you die."

CHAPTER 7

THE ROOM IS SO quiet that I can hear the clock in the corner ticking away. Delphine takes a deep breath. "Well, ladies, I think that's enough for tonight. Vivien and Lucille will take you to your rooms. They will also instruct you on what to wear and where to meet in the morning."

Vivien and Lucille are like copies of Delphine, all middle-aged women with slightly graying hair tied back in a bun and donning puffy maroon dresses with white lace stitched around the collars. I start for the left staircase, the other girls all following.

"Poppy, could you stay behind, please?" Delphine instructs.

A nervous tension coils in my stomach. "Sure."

Joanna stands at my side. "Do you want me to stay with you?"

"You will join the other girls, Joanna. You have nothing to fear from me. I am no wolf."

Joanna sniffs. "No, just the mother of the most high."

I have no idea what she means, but Delphine glares at her. "Go on upstairs. I'll send Poppy up in a few minutes."

Joanna gives my hand a squeeze, then barrels up the stairs after everyone else. I look down at my dirty boots because even though this woman isn't a shifter, she still makes me nervous. I've ruined her perfectly mopped floor.

She sets a hand on my shoulder. "I was given a list of all the girls who were coming, and your name wasn't on it."

I swallow. "I know. My sister Willow was supposed to come."

"And why didn't she?"

"She slapped Anders after he . . . after he . . . touched her inappropriately."

"I see. And so he killed her?" She says it like it's the natural response to being slapped, like there's no surprise my sister was killed.

"Yes." I bite back the words I want to say, things about justice and decency. I don't know that I can trust this woman. I probably can't.

"Your sister and you were twins?"

I jerk my head up. "How did you know that?"

"Because otherwise, you wouldn't have been of age."

I catch a regretful expression on her face before she turns and starts up the stairs, lifting her long skirts so she doesn't trip over them. "Come. I will show you to your room."

I follow her, my steps in my clunky boots so much louder than hers.

"Were you and your sister identical?"

"No. Not at all."

"So you are not the same size?"

"She was six inches shorter than me and had a much larger chest."

She was curvy and beautiful, looking like a woman years before I even sprouted breasts. I didn't mind though. I've never cared for unwanted attention. Besides, most of the boys in our village wanted Charlotte.

Except Knox. I hope I get to see him soon even though I know it will be torture. I hope he's okay, that he's alive and doing well in his new role here, whatever it is. What will he say? What will I do? I swallow and push my first love from my mind. It's a lost cause, really. This city is huge, and Knox is one insignificant claimed man.

Madame Delphine continues. "Well, then we are going to have to find you some different clothes because everything we had made was in her size. I'm sure we've got something that will work. I'll have Lucille take your measurements before you go to bed. Now, tomorrow you will wear a black tank top, shorts, white socks, and sneakers. Meet out on the lawn at six. We do physical fitness for an hour every morning. Then you will shower and change into your uniform. It is the black, fitted dress. You will wear stockings and heels."

I wring my hands together, trying not to panic. I've seen heels in old magazines and on the girls who were on the stage, but I'd never worn a pair myself. Willow and I used to laugh at the absurdity of them. Who can walk in those? I'm certain I'll twist my ankle within minutes of putting them on.

We hit the top of the stairs and enter a massive room with squishy couches and several low tables. Shelves filled with books line the front and side walls, and the back wall has wide doors that look like they open onto a porch.

I stroll over to the books and run my fingers along the spines. Maybe Joanna can read some to me. I've never really cared that I couldn't read before, but now I feel as if I've missed something important.

"This is the claimed's sitting room. There are four bedrooms on this floor and four up in the attic. You sleep two to a room. As there are a lot of you this year, the east room on this floor will sleep four. We had a room set up in the basement for two more, but I understand we lost two to the lycans, so we will not have to use that room. You are lucky enough to only have one roommate. Yours is the west chamber on this floor." She points to a door near the porch. "Between you and me, that's the best room." She winks. "Go on in. I'll send Lucille up in a few moments for your measurements, so don't fall asleep just yet."

I stare at the door. There are two small signs with names scrawled on them. One says Charlotte and the other Willow. I squeeze my eyes to fight back the tears.

She's really dead.

And I'm really about to become a shifter babymaker.

"Madame Delphine?" I ask the question before I talk myself out of it. "Those women you were with earlier tonight, last year's claimed, were they living here before us?"

"Yes, dear. It was their year, just as I was in my time many moons ago. And now it is your time. This is the way of things..." Her voice trails off as if in thought, as if she wants to add something else, but then she turns and walks away.

With a deep breath, I push open the door and find Charlotte inside. Her back is to me as she changes into pajamas. She glares at me over her bare shoulder. "A little privacy, please?"

I can't help but snort as I turn to face the wall. "You didn't seem concerned about privacy when you pulled your bodice down to show off your cleavage to the betas."

She laughs bitterly. "Judging me now will only make you a hypocrite later." She brushes past me. Our room has lavender paper fastened to the walls, two small white beds piled high with cotton bedding, a small chest of drawers at the end of each, and a closet where Charlotte is busy flipping through a rainbow of dresses. "I'm going to do whatever I have to in order to survive this place and make it tolerable," she huffs. "Trust me, Poppy, you're going to be right alongside me soon enough."

The scary thing is she might be right.

I take the bed that Charlotte has left for me and open the drawers, finding my own sets of pajamas waiting. The next drawer contains the neatly folded exercise clothes I'm to wear tomorrow morning. Considering how late it must be, that's going to come fast.

A knock thumps on the door, and both Charlotte and I jump. Lucille pokes her head in. "I've come to get your measurements."

She holds up a long wide string with marks on it. She uses it to find the length of my legs, how wide my hips are, and the size of my chest. She marks them all down in a tiny notebook. Not only does she know how to read, but she can write as well. I find it fascinating, and suddenly, I *do* want to learn to read. She takes a few more measurements, and I study as she scratches out each number. I know the numbers, but the letters mean nothing.

"I'll have a uniform for you after physical fitness. Your shorts have a drawstring in them, so they should work even if they aren't the right size. Goodnight, ladies."

She exits the room, and I peer up at the light affixed to the ceiling. I have no idea how to turn it off. It glows a soft yellow, but if I look at it for too long, my eyes start to water.

"Get into your pajamas, and let's go to bed," Charlotte says. "I need to get my beauty rest."

I'm still staring at the light. "But how do we turn it off?" I'm not even sure if we can. The thought of trying to sleep in blinding unnatural light sends a wave of exhaustion rolling over me.

Charlotte rolls her eyes but smiles ruefully. "Madame Vivien showed us how to do it." She walks over to the wall and points to a little white switch. She flicks it, and the room goes instantly dark. It catches me so off guard that I squeal, then giggle, and then Charlotte turns it back on, and I have to give it a try for myself.

A few minutes later, I tire of the electricity enough to change into my pajamas and fall into the bed. I don't think I've ever lived a longer day in my entire life. The darkness is the only familiar thing about this place and I hate it. Charlotte even breathes differently than Willow did. The events of the day catch up to me, replaying themselves over and over in my mind until I eventually drift away into nightmares of lycans and shifters and blood and death and the two bluest eyes that I've ever seen.

CHAPTER 8

"MY SHIRT IS SO much looser than yours," I complain to Charlotte as I pull the drawstring tight on the shorts.

She shrugs. Her clothes fit her perfectly, but my tank top hangs low, and my shorts are so short I can feel a breeze on my cheeks.

"I look ridiculous," I say.

"You do," she agrees with a triumphant smirk, the kind that lets me know, in no uncertain terms, that we are *not* friends. Why did I have to room with her and not Joanna?

Charlotte and I are the last ones out the back door. The field behind the house is vast and dotted with massive oaks reaching out with their gnarled limbs. We had an oak in the middle of our village square. The kids all loved to play on it. Willow and I used to sneak out at night and climb as high as we could. It was there that we shared our hopes and fears. She was scared of what would become of her when she was claimed, and I was scared of what would happen to me when she was gone.

Now, I know how foolish we were to act as if we had any control over our fates.

I spot Joanna and make a beeline for her, leaving Charlotte behind. The distillery girls snicker as I pass, but I ignore them.

Joanna stares at my legs. "Dang, girl, what happened to your shorts?"

"It was my sister who was supposed to be here, not me. She's short."

"And had boobs." She knocks her finger into the armhole of my shirt and gives a tug. "Here, let me fix this for you." She pulls the drawstring out of her shorts—because they fit fine without it—and uses it to bunch my shirt in the back and tie it up. "There. Now none of us can see your bra. Can't help the butt cheeks though."

I tug on my shorts, but it doesn't do anything. "Thanks for helping me with the shirt. My entire wardrobe is pretty much useless."

She points to herself. "Hey, I'm from the textile village, remember? I am good at altering clothing. I can help you, but we'll have to ask for some supplies."

Relief sweeps through me. "Thank you."

"No problem."

Well, Charlotte may be out, but at least I have Joanna. "How's your roommate?" I ask her.

She sniffs. "Her name is Faye, and she's a distillery girl. I hate her."

I'm grateful Charlotte is not one of them, but from the way she's been kissing up to them, I'm not sure if it would've made a difference. She's practically one of them now. She's currently standing in their little huddle, sending dagger-gazes toward Joanna and me. What did we do to them? Nothing. But it doesn't matter.

My heart sinks a little. This place is going to be rough.

Madame Vivien jogs out in front of us. She's short and athletic with silvery-ginger hair tied back in a ponytail and wearing almost the exact same thing as the rest of us instead of that puffy maroon dress the other house mothers wear. In spite of her age, she's incredibly fit and toned. So are most of the women from my village back home, but she doesn't have the hardness around the edges like they do. I bet her hands are soft as butter.

"Welcome, ladies. I hope you all had a pleasant sleep. I know you had a late night, so I'll go easy on you today, but know that this will not always be the case. We're going to stretch and then jog around the field."

We spread out and all follow along with her stretching. Then Joanna and I set a pace in the middle of the group as we run. The morning air is heavy with humidity but not hot yet, so it's not too bad. Joanna and I chat about our families as we run.

We reach the house and pass it. "One more lap,

ladies," Madame Vivien calls after us. We pass a few distillery girls that were behind us before.

Joanna snorts. "Looks like they've never run before in their lives."

"They probably haven't." Joanna and I both spent our days doing manual labor. I worked in the cotton fields, and she would've been assigned to churn swaths of fabric in giant vats of water and dye. Compared to that, this run is nothing.

We approach the house again, and I slow. Madame Delphine stands on the front steps, but this time, she's not alone. Ryne is with her. His head is dipped low, and he smiles at something she says. It's the first time I've seen him smile in the daylight, and it's beautiful. My stomach flutters—maybe I've taken the sun for granted all my life.

Joanna hits me. "I know he's hot, but stop gawking."

I drop my eyes, my face heating as we approach Madame Vivien. A few of the girls are already there, but many are still far out in the field. I sit on the ground and stretch out my legs. Joanna crouches next to me. "Don't look, but he's staring at you."

I quickly glance up under my eyelashes. Sure enough, it's like he's studying me. There's no anger in his eyes nor attraction—there's curiosity. "Why?" I whisper to Joanna.

She snorts. "Probably because of your shorts."

I flush and stand, moving behind her. Ryne tears his

eyes away from me, kisses Madame Delphine on the cheek, and escapes back into the house.

I let out a breath. At least, I don't have to hide anymore. The rest of the girls finally return, and Madame Delphine joins Madame Vivien on the field.

Madame Delphine makes eye contact with each one of us. Did she hold my gaze a few seconds longer than everyone else's? "Good morning, ladies. Today begins your training. I know this is all new to you, and while some of you have a good idea exactly what you are training for, most of you don't. In any case, I want to clear up any misconceptions you may have." She stares at the distillery girls, and they all drop their eyes. Perhaps they aren't as well informed as I thought.

"If you are lucky, you will be with me for a year," she continues. "In that year, I will teach you all that is necessary to be a good wife and mother to shifters. You will become physically fit, learn to read, and think logically. You will learn to be obedient, subservient, and submissive to your husband." Those three words are a trigger, taking me right back to when Anders stood over Willow's body and announced them as if they were gospel. "You will learn to fight in case you must defend your young. You will be trained in the best way to care for and raise a child." She pauses for a long moment as if to drive her point home. "Our traditions go far back, encouraging the betas to enjoy young women who are well rounded and pleasant to be around, but also cultured and elegant. As a lady, you will learn softer things as well, like how to paint and sing. You will learn how to walk properly and how to groom yourselves so that the men will enjoy your appearance." She holds up a finger. "But do not mistake me. Your purity must stay intact until you are given to the wolves, whatever that may look like for you."

I grimace, knowing exactly what she's speaking of. Mama made sure I knew of holding onto my virginity when Knox and I were dating, because he wasn't going to become my husband. And she spoke of it often to Willow since purity was part of the rules for the claimed. The wolves even sent a doctor to our home to check that her virginity was intact before she came to the claiming. She wouldn't have broken her promise though, not when it would have condemned our family and ended up with her dead. Little good it did her.

Joanna crosses her arms and sniffs. "I'm going to be just the opposite," she whispers so that only I can hear her. "I'm not going to be Grady's *lady*."

Madame Delphine glares at her but doesn't acknowledge the comment. "This is a competition, and not all of you will get to spend a full year here. While all of you train, there are only five betas who will take a bride this year. One is already fated to Joanna." Everyone stares as Joanna bristles, and I catch many of the girls shooting her death glares. "That leaves four for the rest of you."

That's nineteen girls vying for four men. My gut

twists to think about what the next year is going to mean for me. If these men want a beautiful lady, then where does that leave me? I like to work outdoors. I'm tall and too thin to have curves. I don't have golden hair or sparkling eyes, and I never say the right thing.

"So we just have to impress a man?" Faye, Joanna's roommate, who I gather is the leader of the distillery girls, juts out her chest. "That's easy."

Madame Delphine tuts. "Sex appeal will only get you so far. You must prove to us that you can be a respectable lady. It's our tradition that the women who marry the betas hold themselves to the highest caliber. Each day, you will find scores posted in the entry hall. These will be given by your teachers. Every three months there will be a festival during the full moon where the two girls with the lowest scores will be cut from training and sent off."

Faye's face turns stony.

"Sent off where?" I ask. I can't believe I just asked that, but I'm riveted and horrified by what she is saying.

Madame Delphine meets my eye. "Many years ago, when the wars first ended, and the packs took over the remaining cities, humans and wolves mated freely so that humans could have protection, and wolves could breed faster. But as the genes mutated and female wolf children became rare, the claiming was established." She takes a deep breath and lets us in on the terrible truth. "Those of you who are not claimed by a beta will be sent to mate with the lower ranks of deltas and gammas. There are far too many of them to be able to pair you off, so you will mate with more than one man, blessing our community with many children."

"But-but how will they know who their father is?" I whisper.

"They don't have a father or a mother. Those children are raised by the pack."

Her words spin in my head. All of this had been hinted at since I left home, but now that I understand exactly what's expected of me, tears spring to my eyes. I look around at all the other girls. I don't stand a chance.

Madame Delphine continues. "You will do your morning chores after your workouts and before you get dressed in your gowns. There is a chart in the hall with the chores listed. Each day, you will rotate responsibilities. They will prepare you for life after this year of training."

Joanna crosses her arms. "Most of us already know how to do chores. Besides, what good are they going to do any of us? We're just going to spend the rest of our lives on our backs with our legs spread."

I gasp at Joanna's boldness. If she weren't fated, would she still talk like this? Somehow, I think she would, and I like that about her. She reminds me so much of Willow.

Madame Delphine gives Joanna a curious stare. "Well, I guess you probably don't need to learn the chores since it is very clear that you are a fated mate and will not have need of the skills that chores will teach you. Grady will see to it that your household has an adequate staff, which you will be expected to manage. But I do hope you'll do your part while you are with us as Grady is not allowed to take you until the next harvest moon. You may be mated, but he still has to convince his alpha that you are right to be a beta wife."

"That's not what Grady said—"

"All marriages come down to the alpha's approval."

Joanna stiffens and shakes her head, but Madame Delphine ignores her.

"As for the necessity of the chores, with the exception of the four other ladies, most of you will be house servants in the hours that you are not. . . how did you put it, Joanna? Ah yes, on your backs." Her expression turns sad. "Which you will be, more often than not."

She purposefully left out the crude part of Joanna's phrase, but still, our purpose here has become terrifyingly clear. There's nothing any of us can do about it but try to keep our scores high and impress a beta enough to become his wife.

We get sent off to our duties for the morning, and unfortunately, Joanna and I are separated. Madame Vivian insists that Joanna go with her to get her hacked-off haircut fixed. I'm paired up with Charlotte and Faye, and we're sent to collect vegetables from the gardens for dinner tonight. We're to wash them and bring them to the kitchen. I wonder if cooking is another skill we will learn this year. I've always been a terrible cook.

I don't mind gardening since I love working with plants and being outside. Maybe instead of being a house servant one day, I can get a job doing that instead. If I focus on that idea, then I don't have to think about the rest of my duties. I purposely keep the idea of mating locked away in my mind. I don't want to think about it. I can't.

"Fated mates," Faye scoffs as she stomps through the garden. "We'll see about that."

Charlotte huffs along with her. I keep my mouth shut and my ears open.

"What are fated mates?" Charlotte asks.

"Apparently it means that she's destined to be with Grady. It's some weird wolf shifter thing, kinda like our idea of soul mates but stronger." Faye is a short and stunningly curvy girl with big, fawn-like brown eyes and long curly auburn hair. Her looks kind of remind me of Willow, if Willow were to spew venom from her mouth every time she talked. "But he can't choose her until next year, and he has to convince Prince Ryne that she's good enough to be a beta wife." She chuckles low. "And a lot can happen in a year, if you know what I mean."

Charlotte nods.

I whip around, waving the carrots in my hands as I growl at her, "Is that supposed to be some kind of threat?"

Faye glares. "Maybe it is, and maybe it's not. Either way, it's none of your business."

"Joanna is my friend, so that makes it my business."

Faye laughs, turning her insults on me. "You're never going to be selected by a beta." She runs her eyes up and down my body. "Shifters like their women with something to love and hold onto, you know? Like actual boobs and a butt. You might as well be one of the claimed boys. You're so flat-chested."

Charlotte laughs, and my face burns hot. Part of me is hurt by Faye's harsh words, but more than that, I'm upset that Charlotte is going along with this. She's the only person I have left from home. She's my roommate, and I still wanted her to be my friend. Despite the evidence to the contrary, I was clinging to the hope, as stupid as that was. Well, that hope is gone now.

"You don't know what you're talking about," I say, trying not to sound defeated.

"Really?" Faye pops her hip. "The shifters have had tons of interaction with my village for years because they like us better than the rest of you." She juts out her full chest and runs a hand down her perfect hair as if to make her point. "We have good genes." She winks at Charlotte. "But I think you have a great shot, hon. You have the best hair of any girl this year, and your eyes are so pretty. You really stand out."

"Thanks," Charlotte beams.

"Let's take these inside. Ryne's in there." Faye

brushes past me and snatches the pile of carrots right out of my hands as she goes, plopping them into her basket. She opens the garden gate for Charlotte and slams it closed before I can follow.

I glare, but she just tosses her hair over her shoulder and leaves me to manage the rest of the gardening alone. No wonder Joanna hates her. I hate her too. And not only do I have to live with her and girls like her for the next year, but I have to compete with them to get a mate. If I fail, my life will be miserable. I gaze down at myself, judging my body and finding it severely lacking. Maybe she's right. Maybe I don't stand a chance.

THE RIVER IS much sleepier along the bend where the manicured lawn of the estate kisses the water, nothing like it was back where Devansh jumped in. Here it's actually quite peaceful, even though it makes me think of him and wonder if he's alive. I shake the depressing thought from my head, pushing ahead of the rest of the group, and focus on the sunrise as it casts a gorgeous golden glow across the landscape.

We've started off another day with a morning run, and today I use it to collect my thoughts. We're a week into training, and I'm still the fastest one here. Exercise is the one thing I'm actually decent at. Joanna is a close second, so I slow down to her pace. Being the fastest probably isn't a good thing, considering I'm a gangly lightweight with muscles and hands that look like they're used to manual labor. Those traits aren't attractive to the beta wolves picking out a mate, so what good is any of it going to do me here?

Still, I let myself enjoy this one thing I have over the other girls. I'm strong, fast, and I love the feel of blood pumping through my veins. The sun warms my skin in the exact same way it did in the cotton fields back home. If I were to close my eyes right now, I could fool my mind into thinking I was there instead of here. The first smile in days creeps onto my lips.

Two hands shove my back, and I lose my footing, tripping over my feet and plummeting into the river. The cold water shocks me and fills my mouth and nose. I come up sputtering, desperate to get the water clear. After a terrible coughing fit, I stand in the shallow water and find Joanna in it right next to me. Mud drips down her face and clings to her short hair. If she looks like a drowned rat, then what do I look like?

"Who did that?" she screams angrily, but it's useless. The group of girls has passed us, and every single one of them is laughing hysterically. Somehow, over the last few days, it's become the two of us against the eighteen of them. Except Joanna is fated to Grady, so even though she's got my back, sometimes I feel like it's me against the world.

I've never been so lonely.

I climb the steep shore, and Joanna and I help each other out of the water. Mud suctions to my shoes, and some of it runs down my arms and legs.

"Let's go get changed," I grumble. At least Joanna's hair looks cute in the short cut. Madame Vivien did a good job fixing it. Mine is a knotted mess from the river water.

By the time we make it back to the house, the rest of the girls are waiting on the lawn, but they're not alone. The betas are here. Ryne too.

"Great. Perfect timing," I sigh.

"What happened?" Grady growls, stalking toward us like Joanna is in mortal danger and not simply covered in muddy water. "Are you okay? Who did this?" He cups her face and peers into her eyes as if he's already madly in love with her.

She scoffs and shoves him away. "Who says anyone did it? I fell into the river."

He glowers at her. "No one falls into the river by accident."

"I do," she spits out, running her shaking hands over her hair.

Grady turns on me and grips me hard by the shirt. "Did you do this to her? You two get in a fight or something?"

I can't breathe.

Joanna claws at his arm. "She didn't do anything. She's my friend, you idiot."

Grady is ripped from me and thrown to the ground. Ryne stands over him, his eyes blazing with anger. Then he turns that glare at me, and I feel as if the earth just swallowed me whole. He takes a few deep breaths and reaches out to help Grady up. "You know you can't hurt any of the girls. Don't be foolish."

Grady brushes off his pants. "Sorry. I got carried away." He meets my eye. "I apologize, friend of Joanna. What's your name?"

"Poppy," I whisper. "And it's okay."

Although, it's not really okay.

He pats me on the back. "So we're good." He waggles his eyebrows and falls back into line with the other betas. Anders watches me with hungry eyes. Ryne sniffs and scrunches his face as if I smell like a swamp. I'm sure I do.

He grumbles something under his breath that I can't hear and addresses the group. "This is a competition. We like competition. We encourage it. But that said, we don't tolerate sabotage, especially if it puts someone's life at risk. Do you understand?"

The girls agree in unison. Faye's shout of yes is heard above the crowd. I roll my eyes. I'm certain she was the instigator.

Ryne turns on me. "You don't agree, Poppy?"

"Oh, I do," I croak. "It's not like I pushed myself into the river."

"I thought you fell." His eyes flick to Joanna.

She stiffens.

"That's what I meant. We fell." I meet his eyes in

defiance and immediately regret it. The ocean blue color is now stormy with frustration.

He steps back. "Another thing we don't tolerate is lying." He points to the house. "Now go get changed, and, Madame Delphine, please deduct points from Poppy's score today."

I gasp. Are you kidding me? I glare right back at Ryne, matching his indignation with my own. I don't give a crap that he's attractive or that because he's the alpha, I'm naturally drawn to him. This hot and cold attitude is confusing and rude, not that there has been a whole lot of hot except for a few lingering looks. Maybe it's in my head, and he's just cold.

If I were brave like Willow or Joanna, I'd challenge him. But I don't like talking to the wolves, especially not the alpha. I know I have to get used to this, and later in the year, we're even going to have to go on dates with the betas so they can get to know us better, but right now I doubt I'll get that far. I'm pretty sure I won't make the first cut. I really am terrible at all this, and considering those deducted points will now put me at the bottom of the leaderboard, I don't think I'll be able to fool any man into wanting me. And now that Ryne seems to have it out for me, I'm in big trouble.

I brush past him and try not to blush as the five betas stare after me. Joanna has been altering my clothing, and Madame Delphine has brought in a few new things for me, but the exercise gear is still the same ill-fitting and overly revealing stuff that was made for my sister. I can practically feel Anders's gaze on my butt, but I'd rather die than mate with him. If he picks me, I'll refuse him. I don't even know if I can, but I will, even if it means death. So, who do I have left? Three men who I haven't met yet and who haven't looked twice at me.

Joanna and I go up to change. Each day we're assigned our outfit—usually a dress—and today is no different. I pout at the hot fabric and then hurry back down the stairs to join the others. Joanna is waiting at the door.

"I can't afford to lose any more points today," I sigh.

"I know. I'm sorry." She's upset because there's nothing she can do to help me. "I understand if you don't want to be my friend anymore."

"What?" I stop and turn on her.

"You'd probably have better luck if you took Faye's side. You know, like your roommate did. I'm just going to bring you down. I'd be dead right now if that idiot Grady hadn't decided I'm his mate." Her facial expression is calm and collected, but her eyes shine.

"First off, Charlotte's a brown-noser. Secondly, Faye's a jerk. And third, there's a reason that you're the only friend I have here." I pull her into a tight hug. "I wouldn't trade you for any of those girls." When she hugs me back, I can feel her worries begin to ease.

She might be right, but I can't bring myself to ditch her just to save my own skin. It probably wouldn't help me anyway. I already know how this ends. Besides, I really like her, and I wish I could be half as brave as she is.

"You know," I go on, "maybe I can be a servant in your household with Grady." That's when I'm not being forced into mating, of course.

"Don't think that way," Joanna hisses. "We're going to get out of here before any of that happens."

How she thinks we're going to get away is beyond me, but I nod and follow her the rest of the way down the stairs. I'll let her worry about escaping. Right now, I need to worry about getting my scores up.

We get through our morning chores and are sent back outside. When we walk out onto the lawn, and I see what our activity is for the day, my heart drops. Will I never catch a break?

Twenty art easels have been set up in the grass. Back in my village, we have an artist named Laurel. She always manages to find bits of charcoal to draw with and makes paint out of plants and crushed stone. Every home in our village has a painting from her hung on the wall. Once a week, she teaches the village children how to draw, paint, and sculpt. I always went to her classes because it was a break from our normal labor, but to say I'm a terrible artist would be a massive understatement.

Everyone always "oohed" and "aahed" over Willow's art, while Laurel would put a hand on my shoulder and say, "Maybe next week we'll find your talent." I'd laugh, thinking it was nice of her to imagine there was any artistic talent hidden somewhere in me for her to find. Years of lessons, and she never found an ounce. But back then, it didn't matter. It was just for fun. And now it does—I certainly won't be moving up the scoreboard after today's lesson, that's for sure. Too bad running doesn't count for much. It should. They were the ones who said they wanted women who could defend their young as well as be proper ladies.

Madame Lucille stands in the middle of the easels and waves us toward her. "I will be your art instructor. Once a week, you will spend a few hours with me, learning how to paint. The betas enjoy the finer things in life, and they'll like mates who can create beautiful things for their homes."

My eyes flick to where the betas are grouped up on the porch, observing us from above like overlords. Grady is taken, which leaves Anders, Justin, Cade, and Nico. They're attractive enough, but every time I look at them, all I can see is what they represent.

The girls hang on Lucille's every word. Charlotte has a small smile on her face. Most of the girls here have probably never even picked up a paintbrush before. Charlotte and I are at an advantage, thanks to Laurel. Well, Charlotte is, but not me. I might even be at a disadvantage because I already know how bad I'm going to be, and my hands are starting to shake.

"Today, I would like to see what kind of artist you

are so I can help cultivate your natural talents. Perhaps you are good with portraits, or maybe your skills lie in landscapes and nature. Others of you will lean toward the more abstract arts. Paint me a picture today that tells me who you are."

Joanna and I snag easels right next to each other. "Have you ever painted before?" I ask her.

"Not paint, but I can draw. I'm a fairly skilled designer, and if I hadn't been claimed, I would've probably been brought closer to the city anyway to design dresses and things for the beta wives." She digs out the colored pencils from the basket next to the easel and starts to sketch.

I study my own basket. There are several different kinds of art materials. Laurel would be in heaven. I wish I could give the basket to her somehow. She'd do it justice, and then I could go back to running, the only thing I'm even remotely good at, the only thing that clears my head and allows me to forget where I've ended up. But no. With a resigned sigh, I find a tube of black paint and grab a wide brush. I smear the paint right on the canvas. Then I dig the brush into it, jerking to the left, leaving a wide swath of black paint. Then I paint up and down. Anger courses out of me, and I dig the brush in harder.

I smear red onto the canvas. Willow is dead.

Then I do blue. I'm doomed to a life of whoring against my will.

Next comes yellow. Ryne has it out for me.

Then purple. So does Faye and her gang and maybe even Charlotte.

I brush this way and that, not really caring how it looks. Tears start, and I can barely see what I'm doing.

Willow is dead.

Dead.

Dead.

Dead.

A hand falls on my wrist. "Poppy, stop." Joanna jerks my hand away from the canvas, and muddy brown paint splatters all over her shirt. I drop the paintbrush and fall on her shoulder, sobbing.

CHAPTER 10

THE DAYS BLUR TOGETHER, much like the paint did on my canvas during that first art lesson, and really, every subsequent lesson since. I'm depressed—it's not something I've ever experienced before. Oh, I certainly thought I was after Knox was claimed, and I definitely thought I was during the final weeks with Willow, but nothing has even come close to this level of despair. It's like I'm living with a knife in my stomach that nobody but me can see. My life has become hopeless and painful and numbing all at the same time, and that knife twists deeper each and every day.

I should be home, grieving my sister with my family. I should be out in the fields with Papa or baking bread with Mama or telling bedtime stories to Evan. Instead, I've spent the last two weeks since that art lesson trying to force myself into a mold that I'll never fit.

It's pointless.

"Are you not even going to get out of bed?" Charlotte snaps at me early one morning while shimmying into her workout gear. Her back is to me, but even in the shadows, I can tell her body is perfectly curved and exactly what the betas want in a wife. I'm pretty sure she's going to end up with the tall blonde beta named Justin, based on the way he looks at her, which is fine by me, but I still grumble and roll away.

"Joanna is worried about you, you know," she huffs. "She thinks you could get a beta if you were to actually try. Not that I think that, but you know, she does. Attitude is everything, and this mopey one of yours is not attractive."

I do know that. I know that I'm a mess. I know that I'm not trying. And that Joanna thinks I have a chance. But the woman is also under the delusion that we're going to be able to run away and somehow survive out in the wilds, so it's not like her judgment can be trusted.

"Tell them I'm sick," I finally murmur. I roll back over to face the wall. I usually enjoy this part of the day because I love physical exercise, but it's only one measly hour, and then hell starts. I can't be bothered anymore.

I may as well give up now. Either way, I'll be shipped off to the mating house come the Wolf Moon Festival in January. I've literally been near or at the bottom of the leaderboard every day since we arrived here. I close my eyes and drift back to sleep. I dream of home, but it's wrong. Nobody can see me, and it's like I never existed.

Rough hands shake me awake. "What?" I sputter, trying to pry my eyes open. My body is heavy, and my mind is filled with cobwebs.

"Come on." Madame Delphine leans over me. "You have to get moving."

"I can't today. I don't feel well."

She presses her hand to my forehead and tuts. "You're fine. Now, come on, there's something I want to show you."

"If you take a special interest in me, it's only going to make the other girls hate me more," I groan.

"That's funny because I didn't think you cared."

She's right. I've been too sad to care what *anyone* thinks.

Madame Delphine is obviously not going to take no for an answer, so I peel myself from my mountain of warm blankets. She leaves, and I dress in my gown for the day—a pretty navy-blue one with a sweetheart neck-line—clean my face and teeth, and brush out my long hair. When she returns with a shiny green apple, I take it because it's the only breakfast I'm going to get this late in the day. I don't even know what time it is. We head downstairs, and I half-expect her to lead me to the class-room where the other women are taking a singing lesson—another talent that's escaped me—but she doesn't. We walk right past their closed door and out the front.

A couple of the betas are hanging out on the porch, and my face reddens because they must know I'm being forced to get out of bed today. I feel ashamed, and I hate that feeling and refuse to own it. They go silent, watching as she directs me into a waiting car. It's black and shiny and belongs to Ryne. I've seen him dropped off in it a couple of times, but never thought I would get to ride in it. When I slide into the backseat, and he's not there, I'm thankful but also a tad disappointed. He must be in the house somewhere. Why is he here so much? He's not a beta, but I guess he's invested in making sure his men end up with suitable wives.

Madame Delphine slides into the backseat next to me and shows me how to strap myself in safely, using what she calls a seatbelt. It's restrictive and cuts into my neck. My stomach rumbles, so I bite into the apple and look up just as the driver catches my gaze in his mirror. Time slows to a stop.

I know those eyes—those honey-brown eyes—those kind farmers' son eyes.

I fell in love with those eyes.

"Knox," I whisper and cough on the apple chunk.

"Are you okay, child?" Madame Delphine asks, patting me on the back.

Knox looks away. But it's him. *It's him!*

"Fine," I squeak.

I knew there was a possibility that I'd see Knox at some point, but I wasn't expecting it today. My heart beats so loudly that I can hear it thumping in my ears. I drop my eyes, studying my hands. I want to look at him again, but I can't, or we might both get into trouble. It's very likely he has no idea why I'm even here. I wasn't supposed to be. I'm not Willow. Or maybe he's already overheard the whole story. If he is Ryne's private driver, he probably hears a lot. But does Ryne speak of me? Maybe Ryne doesn't even think of me when he leaves here. Knox could be just as stunned right now as I am.

"What do you know about our children?" Madame Delphine interrupts the storm of emotions whirling through me.

"Our children? Are you a shifter then?" I ask without thinking.

She chuckles. "Goodness no, but I did mother one."

"Just one?"

"So you don't really know about their kind at all? I thought they taught you lessons before you came."

"They do, but I wasn't supposed to come, remember? My sister took the lessons, not me."

Madame Delphine pats my hand. "I am sorry about your sister."

"It's not your fault."

"I know, but I hate death of any kind."

This surprises me coming from a woman who teaches girls to be subservient to men.

I stare out the window and watch the shells of houses go by. A few have been cobbled back together, but not many. Mostly, it's just trees and fields of weeds. Part of me would like to clean it up, to make it beautiful, but the shifters don't deserve beauty.

"Anyway," she continues as if my prolonged silence isn't awkward. "How much do you know about the moon virus?"

I clear my throat and try not to meet Knox's gaze even though I want to. I can tell he's looking at me again. "I know that many generations back the humans and supernatural creatures were in a huge war for control of the world. The humans bombed just about everything, trying to get rid of the supernaturals, but it didn't work." I think about the wasteland between my village and the next. "It only made it worse. Humans were close to becoming extinct until they released a lab-created virus." My voice trails off.

"Go on."

"Well, all I know is that it was airborne and lethal, and humans were immune to it. It killed most of the supernaturals off except for the ones that had mostly human blood in their veins—the lycanthropes and the shifters."

"That's correct," she continues. "We believe it was that virus that altered the wolf shifters fertility. They can still procreate, but it doesn't happen frequently, and there's still the problem of only producing male offspring ninety-nine percent of the time. As you can imagine, only having one percent of shifters being born female would eliminate their race pretty quickly if they couldn't breed with humans."

I stiffen and try to push the anger down. "So they created the claiming."

"As a way to protect humans from the growing lycan population and as a way to keep the shifter numbers strong." Her tone isn't defensive. It's matter-of-fact, like of course the claiming only makes sense.

I turn on her. "But why can't all the claimed have one mate? It's not right what they're doing."

Her eyes turn sympathetic, but she still defends the wolves. "You have to understand. Most betas will only have one or two children during a woman's fertile years. That's not enough to keep the pack numbers where we need them to stay protected."

I'm putting the pieces together, finally getting what she's saying, and my stomach is sick with the truth of it. "So they take additional mates..."

"Yes. If a woman has no child by the age of thirty-five, the beta returns to guarding the city and can elect to take another mate whenever he chooses. At that point, he will no longer be married to his first wife and will leave her for his second, or third, and so on."

"And if she does have a child?" I ask.

"Then she is allowed to raise him, but once he comes of age and joins the pack, her time as a mate is done, and the same process continues. Unless of course if they are fated mates, then they will stay together for her lifetime, even if they aren't blessed with children. But those are rare cases. Joanna is the first one I've seen in my five years as house mother."

So she's only been doing this for five years. Interesting . . .

"Then where do the beta wives go after they are no longer good for bearing children?" Maybe I shouldn't be curious about this, but I am.

"They usually take jobs overseeing the children's homes, but a few have other roles in the city. Some manage the girls in the mating houses or run a shop. Others simply live a life of luxury and do nothing. They are not required to work if they are married to the betas, so they only do if they wish to stay busy." She frowns. "In fact, there is a group of them that get together and gossip as if it's their job."

"These are just the beta wives, right? What about the rest of the girls?"

I have to know because that is likely my fate. It's good to know that I won't be stuck doing it forever. I look up front to where Knox is driving, wondering what he's thinking of all of this. I wish I could include him in our conversations, could get his opinion on everything, or even gain just one look to know his thought process.

But he doesn't look back at me again.

"They stay in service until they're no longer able to

bear children," she explains. "Then most of them go work with the children, helping to raise them in community houses and sometimes acting as wet nurses for the infants. It's assumed they will birth children from the lower ranks of gamma and deltas, but there are betas who frequent the mating houses as well, so who knows, really." I can't help but grimace at that. She's saying that these men get to have a wife and countless mistresses at the same time, and it's fine because it's in the name of growing the pack. The whole thing makes my heart hurt, especially since those children aren't even raised by their own mothers. "Mating house girls are much more fruitful than beta wives, with most having twelve to fifteen children in their time."

My jaw falls open. I remember the sounds Mama made when she birthed Evan. It was painful, bloody, and it quite honestly scared me. I've never known any family back in the village to have that many children. "How is that possible if the shifters are so infertile?"

"Most girls have four to five partners a day." Her voice sounds regretful, but I can't quite be sure if she honestly cares, considering her job is to prepare us for these horrors. "It doesn't take long at that rate. Once they are pregnant, they go live in a birthing home with other pregnant girls, where they are pampered to no end."

"Oh, so now that she's pregnant, she has value to you?" I snort. "Got it."

"A woman *always* has value here," she sighs. "But we

want to protect those babies. Our future safety depends on them growing up into warriors. Don't forget what the wolves do for the humans out in the villages."

I bite my tongue, because all I can think of is what Anders did for my family.

"After the child is born, the woman is given a month of recovery time and then must return to the brothel, where, if she is lucky, she will only be a month or two before she is pregnant again."

"Why do you do this?" I can't help the question from spilling out.

"It's exactly as I said. We need to grow the pack for everyone's protection."

"Fast enough to require forced breeding?" I haven't felt much besides grief lately, but right now, I definitely feel anger, and that anger is forcing life into me again, so I welcome it.

"The lycans—"

"Are there *really* that many lycans?" I cut her off. The first I'd ever seen of one was at the claiming cere- mony. And yes, it was huge, but there were countless shifters ready to take it and its companions down.

"There are," she says, her voice growing cold and frustrated, "and they are building their army every full moon." She unbuckles her seatbelt as the car slows to a stop. "Enough about that. We're here."

CHAPTER 11

I MISS MY FATHER. He described cities like this to us kids, his stories having been passed down through the generations. Of course, he'd never seen one in person, but hearing him speak so confidently of them always made me wonder if maybe he had. He often talked of the tall shiny structures reaching into the sky like glass fingers, exactly like these. I gaze up at the blue and gray and brown buildings that seem to reflect every color of the rainbow and try not to smile. It's unlike anything I've ever seen before, and it makes me feel small and insignificant but also excited all at the same time. We'd seen so little of the city when we arrived. I hadn't realized we'd missed so much.

It's only when Knox opens my door and takes my hand to help me out of the car that I'm knocked back into reality. He squeezes once and then drops it, turning away. Meanwhile, a million memory seeds bloom within me. Growing up with him flashes behind my eyes—our few school classes together and how he hated the art workshops same as me, working the fields next to his large family of boys, the first time he showed interest *in me* with that dimpled smile and those kind brown eyes, our first kiss beneath the summer willow trees, the first dance around the community bonfire, and the day I had to say goodbye . . .

And now, he's here and a slave, and soon I will be too.

"This way, dear." Madame Delphine threads her arm through mine. Thankfully she's missed the connection Knox and I have. Will he and I ever get to talk at all? "It's time for you to see why you need to get out of bed each morning and fight for a beta." She begins pulling me toward one of the buildings.

I catch Knox's expression as I go. His face has gone gray, like he's about to be sick. So am I, for that matter. I don't want to be mated to a beta or sent to a mating house. I want to fall back into Knox's arms and forget about this nightmare. I want us to go home, to be normal teenagers.

I hadn't realized how much I missed him until now.

Several cars pass by, and I jump. Even after riding in one, I'm not used to how fast they go. Madame Delphine chuckles. "I remember when I first arrived at the city. Everything terrified me. You'll get used to it."

We step inside the shiny doors, and I'm immediately disappointed. The only thing inside is a long, bright white hallway with a few glass doors along the walls. Madame Delphine walks swiftly through the hall, and I peek through the glass. All I see are a few women sitting at desks and shuffling papers around.

At the end of the hall are four wide metal doors. Madame Delphine pushes a button, and there is a loud ding, but nothing happens. "What's that?" I ask.

"An elevator. It will take us up to other floors."

I turn the foreign word around in my head in examination, wondering how an elevator is going to work.

"What are those women doing back there?" I question.

"They are coordinators. They make sure that every child is matched with a caretaker and plan the children's schedules and meals."

I think that would be a job I could do someday. It certainly would be better than raising children who aren't my own. Though it probably requires reading, and I'm not good at that. Maybe if I'm able to stay in the house longer, I'll be able to learn.

There is another loud ding, and the doors in front of us slide open. We step inside what appears to be nothing more than a tiny metal room, and Madame Delphine pushes a button with the number four on it. The doors close, trapping us inside. The little box of a room lurches up, and I grip the nearest handrail as my weight shifts. Madame Delphine smiles.

In no time at all, the box stops moving, and the doors slide open to a cacophony of sound. I press my hands to my ears as we step out. The whole space is wide open with tons of equipment for children to play on.

Little boys are everywhere, laughing and playing. A few are tussling, and a woman runs over to break it up. If I had to guess, I'd say they were all around the age of three or four. And to think, they're all shifters, all going to grow up to be part of this wolf pack.

Madame Delphine puts a hand to her chest. "Goodness me, I forgot how loud they were at this age."

I nod and lower my hands. "My little brother was loud, but there was only one of him." I hate that I'm thinking of him in the past tense, but chances are I'll never see him again.

An adorable curly-haired boy runs up to Madame Delphine and wraps his arms around her legs. "Hi, lady!" he looks up to her. She pats him on the head, and then he jumps over to me and does the same to my legs. I laugh down at him and smile while a woman approaches.

"Madame Delphine, what brings you to our home?" The woman curtsies a bit and pries the little boy away from my legs. I have to admit I wish I could get another hug.

"I'm here to show one of my girls how the children

are raised. I thought she might appreciate it. Poppy, meet Nana Eliza. She and I were in the same claiming year."

"Oh, how nice. Were you a beta wife before coming here?"

Eliza's eyes go sharp. "No."

I'm instantly ashamed of my assumption. Madame Delphine doesn't say anything. I figured since they are friendly, they'd run in the same circles during their child-bearing years, and she must have been a beta wife. But apparently not. "Oh, I'm sorry."

Nana Eliza doesn't have time to stand around and talk. There are so many children here and so few care-takers that she's immediately pulled back to her job. We circle the large playroom, talk to a few of the little boys, and then go back to the elevator.

This time Madame Delphine pushes the number for fifteen. "We group the children born of each mating house together. They're then separated by age. Once they age up a year, they go to live on the next level. Each level has sleeping, eating, bathing, and learning quarters for the children. Age fifteen is the last year they'll live in this particular building. At sixteen they are assigned delta or gamma class. They will join the army or be given other assignments and move to new quarters. Those first two years are grueling work, but it's how the boys become men. And at age eighteen, they're permitted to begin mating with the women in the mating houses. They will mate until they grow old and pass away, though many don't make it to old age because of the lycans."

So that's why she brought me here. To see who my potential mates will be one day. I shiver to think of just how old these shifters can get, not wanting to imagine what mating with someone old enough to be my father or grandfather would be like.

The door opens, revealing how high up we are. The view of the city from here makes me want to jump back into the elevator. Just like before, it's noisy, and boys are everywhere.

Much, much older boys.

They're all standing around in what appears to be an open empty room, save for a few floor mats. If I could count them, I'd guess there'd be over fifty boys, and they all turn to look at me at the same time. I want to disappear.

"Hey, pretty mama," one of the closest ones calls out loud enough for everyone to hear. He waggles his eyebrows and then grabs his crotch. "Wanna practice on me?"

"That's enough, Klein," an older man barks out, stomping forward and whopping the smirking kid across the back of the head. "Talk to the women that way in front of me again, and you'll earn yourself a lashing."

I swallow hard and glare at Klein, but when he catches me looking, he blows me a kiss.

"Madame Delphine." The older man steps forward

to shake her hand. "To what do we owe the pleasure of your company?"

"One of my girls needs a lesson in how our pack works." She gestures toward the boys. "Carry on. Poppy and I will observe from here."

The man nods once and returns to instructing the boys in combat methods. And then two by two, he directs them to shift and fight each other on the mats. When they begin stripping down so they can shift without ruining their clothes, my cheeks heat, and I drop my gaze to my feet.

What comes next is bloody. And loud.

I didn't expect it to be so awful. They growl and snarl at each other, claws and fangs sinking deep into their opponents. They're evenly matched and don't hold anything back as they battle one another. For the first time, I wonder if wolves within the same pack kill each other. Dominance is *everything*.

I press myself against the cool elevator doors. "Can we go, please?"

"Do you see now, child?" Madame Delphine says. "One way or another, you will bear the wolves' children. In one case, you will get to raise them and love them as your own. In another, you won't even know them. They grow up here and belong to the pack."

I nod but don't say anything. There's nothing else to add.

I hate that the betas are so special to warrant a real

family unit while the rest are raised in groups, but I can see now that's all part of the control. Make a wolf beholden to the pack and his fellow wolves his brothers, and he'll do anything for them, even die for them. The pack becomes more important than family when the pack *is* the family.

So why let the betas keep their children?

There must be a reason, but I'm still not sure what it is.

The doors open, and I stumble back into a broad chest. Large hands steady me, and I turn back to stare up into the blue eyes that have infiltrated my dreams each night since the harvest moon. "Mother, what are you doing bringing her up to this floor?" Ryne hisses. "You said you were taking her to see the children."

Mother?

Ryne's warm hands stand me upright, and I turn to take Ryne and Madame Delphine in, suddenly very aware of the resemblance between them. Madame Delphine is Ryne's mother—the *alpha's* mother—and I had no idea.

"She hasn't been trying."

"I'm aware of that."

"So she needs to know exactly what she's getting herself into," Madame Delphine continues coolly, not the least bit phased by the alpha. "Quite frankly, all the girls do."

Ryne glares for a moment, then motions for her to

join us in the elevator. When she does, his face goes stony. "Fine, Mother. If that's what you want, then let's take her across the street, shall we?"

Madame Delphine stiffens.

"What's across the street?"

They don't answer me.

CHAPTER 12

"I'M GOING to head home. You two go alone," Madame Delphine insists. "Knox will have time to get me there and back before you're through."

My eyes widen. She's leaving me alone with him? Ryne softens and runs a hand through his black hair. It tumbles back around his shoulders. "Maybe she's learned her lesson and doesn't need to see what's in there. I can send her back with you." He turns on me. "If you promise to try harder."

Something about that causes a fire to rise within me. "You wanted me to see what's across the street, so show me what's across the street."

"She needs to see it for herself," Madame Delphine cuts in and levels a hard look at Ryne. "That is your fate if you do not win a beta." Her unreadable expression and the fact that she said words clearly meant for me while looking at her son is confusing, but I don't ask questions. Not when I don't know if I want to know the answers. If anything, today has made things worse, not better. I think I would rather die than live among these beasts.

"Of course, Mother. I'll bring her home when we're done." His tone is regretful, but nobody changes their mind, and so I follow Ryne across the street.

We enter another tall shiny building, and my ears are immediately assaulted by the loud music. This isn't like the music we made ourselves back in the village. This is something else entirely, something foreign and wild. The lights are dim, but I can still clearly see most of the vast room. I immediately wish I couldn't. Girls are everywhere and in various states of undress. A few wear no tops at all. Mother would be horrified by all of this— most people would! I desperately want to go home and forget this nightmare exists.

Ryne puts a hand on my back and bends low to whisper in my ear. I can't help but feel secure under his touch, and I hate myself for that too.

"This is the Broad Street Mating House. It's the worst of the lot. Don't leave my side while we are in here. My wolves are allowed to do almost anything they want with women inside this particular brothel. They won't bother you if you are with me though."

It's too hot in here. A bead of sweat trickles down the back of my neck. Ryne leads me through the crowded room to an empty round booth near the back. He slides in, and I go after him. I sit a little apart from him, but close enough that he could protect me if I needed him to.

Ryne waves down a woman in a black uniform. "I want a scotch and a glass of wine." The woman is older than the other women here—too old for bearing children. That must be why she's been assigned this job. She nods and disappears.

"What do you think?" Ryne asks.

I take in the scene. There's a lot of dancing or standing around, and with bodies so close together, it's sometimes hard to tell where one ends and the next begins. Most of the men have women hanging all over them, as if they want to be with these vile men. My heart hurts.

"I don't understand why the girls would go after the wolves. I wouldn't."

The waitress comes back with the drinks, and he thanks her. Ryne hands me the glass of wine. I've never had anything with alcohol in it before—Mama wouldn't allow it—but I don't tell Ryne that. I just take a sip of the bitter liquid. I don't like it.

"Actually, you would. Most of the girls want to get pregnant."

"Why?"

"Probably to get a break from here," he mutters and downs his drink.

Couples come and go from various doors, and I

shudder to think what is happening behind the closed ones.

We don't say anything more. I just sip at my wine and watch. That's what he wants me to do, isn't it? To see what will happen to me if I don't try harder. A lot of the women are laughing, but they have dead, soulless eyes. The men mostly seem pleased with all the attention. It's not a life I want, not at all. I want to be in control of my body and my fate. I want love and a real family. I want to work in the fields and go to bed feeling accomplished with dirt under my fingernails. I want to grow old without ever having known this place existed. But I was born a human girl in a shifter's world, and that will never be the case.

The wine leaves my body feeling calm, and I start to think that this wouldn't be so bad, to be desired by so many. And then I shake my head. I can't think like that. It's a trap.

"I think if I were here, I wouldn't dress like the others," I announce.

Ryne eyes me, the blue seeming to glow in the darkness. "What do you mean?"

"I would cover myself from head to toe and hide in a corner. Then I wouldn't have to do anything or get pregnant to get out of here."

Ryne scowls. "That would be worse for you."

"Why?"

"Not all of my wolves are gentlemen. Some like to be

rough, they like to be challenged, and they seek out women who are hiding. Sometimes the new women try to hide like you said, but after a few days, they're acting just like any of the others in here."

Almost as if to illustrate Ryne's point of wolves not being gentlemen, one storms across the room and rips a woman out of the arms of the man whose lap she's sitting on. The man with the empty lap growls and stands, fur rippling on his arms, but the first man towers over him. They circle each other, and it reminds me of the teenagers from across the street. This is a show of dominance more than it's about one particular female. The man who lost the girl finally backs down, and the other throws the woman over his shoulder, stalking from the room with her. She doesn't fight him.

Ryne waves the waitress down. "Another scotch and wine, please."

"Why didn't the other guy fight?" I ask.

"Because he's a gamma, and the other is a beta. Gammas can challenge a beta for their place in the pack, but they rarely win. If and when they lose, they'll either be killed in the fight or sent out to the wilds to try and make it as a lone wolf. We don't survive on our own. We're not meant to be separated from our kin."

And nobody survives in the wilds.

I think about the beta man and the rough way he handled the woman, yanking her around like a piece of property. I'm glad he's not one of the monsters I'm supposed to compete for this year. "And to think, a lot of the girls at the house believe your betas only take one mate. Oh, to be married to a beta, what a dream." I roll my eyes.

He snorts, "They only take one wife at a time, that's true. But many betas are unmated, so they visit the brothels just like the gammas. And while they usually stop while they're married, some do not."

"Maybe you can answer a question for me." He hums to himself and I'm not sure if that's a yes or a no, but I ask it anyway. "Why let the betas have families at all?"

He goes still. "It's a perk for the betas and a goal for the new woman."

"Right. Some goal. And what about you, Ryne? Do you visit the brothels?" I have no idea why I'm being so bold. It must be the wine. Or maybe it's the fact that I'm pissed off.

"I do." He rakes a hand through his midnight hair and gives me a challenging look. My mouth pops open, and I suddenly feel a flicker of betrayal, which is ridiculous. I have no claim to this alpha. He catches my sour expression. "I do what is expected of me, but I am also a man. Your judgment doesn't bother me."

Then why does it sound like it does bother him? "And what kind of man are you? Do you violently take the women, or do you let them come to you?"

The low red light from the lamp above us shines on

the black hair that hangs around his shoulders, framing his face in lurid shadows. He levels a heated gaze on me, and it does things to me that I'd rather not admit. "I take what I want, Poppy. Don't you ever forget that."

"You didn't answer my question."

"No, I'm never violent with women."

"And what about allowing others to be violent with them? You're the alpha. You make the rules, don't you?" I fold my arms over my chest and lean back into the padding of the booth. I need to put space between us.

A sardonic frown tugs at his lips. "I don't make the rules. I enforce them."

"Alright, then who makes the rules?"

"My father." He sighs heavily. "The alpha king."

It never occurred to me that his father was still alive, considering Ryne's the alpha of this pack, but then again, Ryne is a prince, so it would stand to reason that his father is a king. "And where's your father?"

"So many questions." He chuckles darkly, takes another sip, and then looks off into the distance as if lost in a daydream. "He runs the Chicago Pack."

"And he's okay with violence toward women?" I'm growing braver by the second. "Your beta killed my sister, and now I'm supposed to pursue him as my future husband. Why do you think I've been so depressed?"

"If you end up here," he snaps. "Anders will have you anyway. He does not care to be loyal to a wife and will continue to frequent the mating houses often." Even though it's what I've been learning today, to hear it so bluntly rocks me to my core. "Your best bet is to go for one of the other three betas choosing brides this year. And yet, I haven't seen you try. Do you even remember their names?"

My face reddens. He has me there. I do know them, but he's put me on the spot, and my mind is more muddled than ever.

"Cade, Nico, and Justin," he spits out.

"I knew that!" I wave at the scene unfolding around us. "But you need us. Without human women, you'd have no pack. So maybe you should punish those of you who kill innocent women." My eyes narrow. "Anders shouldn't get off so easily."

He leans back against the leather bench and stares at me until my stomach twists and tiny hairs dance across my arms. I don't break his gaze. I'm right. I know I'm right.

"Your sister was replaced by you before your arrival, so Anders wasn't punished," he finally replies. "But I assure you that if any of these women in here are killed by one of my wolves, the wolf responsible will be sent to the wilds."

"Anders should be sent to the wilds."

"Anders is the highest-ranked beta and my number two." He tenses. "Be careful to remember who you're talking to."

I glare. "So that's what it's like being an alpha, huh?

You make it okay for someone to murder my innocent sister just because the guy's your little lacky?"

Something unreadable crosses his features, and he turns away. He has nothing to say, probably because he knows I've caught him with the truth. Sometimes the truth hurts, but not as bad as watching a beloved sister be ripped apart by the very thing that was supposed to protect her. I want Ryne to hurt about this, as if that will take away some of my pain.

It won't.

A woman approaches our table. She's tall and pretty, with wide blue eyes and long sleek blonde hair. She wears a tight short skirt and a plunging crop top that shows generous cleavage. Nearly downright modest compared to what everyone else is wearing.

And silly me, I didn't even know clothing like this existed.

She slides into the booth next to Ryne and puts a hand on his chest. "Ryne, we haven't seen you here in forever. Did you come back because you missed me?"

He extracts her hand, and she leans up and bites his ear, trailing kisses along his neck. I look away and stare into my drink, my chest burning. I can't tell if it's jealousy or just embarrassment for him. But also, I kind of hate him right now, so the last thing I want to see is him enjoying himself because of a system that is broken and wrong. And besides, I have absolutely no reason to be jealous. Ryne is the alpha. I'd never land him in any kind of way that would be meaningful. Not that I want to. He's enforcing all of this, after all.

When he kisses her back, hot bile rises to my throat, and I want to claw the two of them apart. What the hell is wrong with me? I do not want Ryne!

A hand slides up my thigh, and I jerk my head up. A man has managed to sit beside me without me even realizing it.

"You are a pretty thing," he says, alcohol hot on his breath.

I close the distance between me and Ryne, sliding an arm behind his back without thinking and gripping his waist with my hand. The only thing to save me here will be if this man thinks I'm with Ryne.

Ryne jerks away from the girl, reaches across me, and grabs the man by the throat. The table topples over, sending our drinks flying. The other girl disappears.

Ryne gets right into the man's face. "Don't you dare touch her. She's with me. Do you understand?"

The man's eyes widen, and he nods. Ryne drops him and holds out his hand to me. "I think we've seen enough. Let's go."

CHAPTER 13

THE NEXT DAY I'm out of bed before Charlotte. I put on my workout gear, head downstairs, and step out into the warm, humid air. Today's exercise is yoga, but I want to get a run in before we start because I always feel better afterward.

I stop dead on the deck. Ryne stands there with Madame Delphine, both talking in low whispers. Neither has noticed me.

"Father would never allow it," Ryne says.

"You can't deny fate. He would be forced to understand."

Ryne gives a low chuckle. "No, he wouldn't."

I step forward loudly so that they don't think I'm eavesdropping, and Ryne spins around. "Poppy, what are you doing here?"

A small thrill goes through me at the way he says my

name, drawing the end out a little. I clench my fists.

"I wanted to get a run in before the day began. That's allowed, isn't it?"

"Of course," Madame Delphine says, stepping aside. I slip past her and Ryne, and I try to ignore their eyes on me as I take off across the field. Soon, I find my rhythm, and all my turbulent emotions disappear.

I finish my second lap and find the rest of the girls already outside stretching, so I go and join Joanna.

"Glad to see you up and at 'em. Whatever they showed you yesterday must've made an impact." She was a little bitter that I wouldn't tell her, but I didn't want to relive the day. All I know is that, in spite of not wanting to be a part of this at all, it's time for me to fight for a beta because the alternative is too horrific. I've got a year to get myself from the bottom of the charts to the top. And I'm going to do it for Willow. For myself. Joanna still talks of running off, and if she finds a way, I'll join her, but I'm not counting on it.

Madames Delphine, Vivien, and Lucille all stand at the bottom of the stairs in tight black tank tops, leggings, and boots. I've never seen Madame Delphine out of a dress. She looks ten years younger, not to mention fierce and deadly. I wouldn't want to get on her bad side.

"Today we have a special training exercise for you. We will take you into the basement. There will be no talking once we enter. Silence is a must, or points will be deducted. This is not the day to test us."

I quickly glance at Joanna, and she raises her eyebrows. We enter the basement through the cellar door, and all fall silent as we descend the stairs. This place has a creepy energy, and I'm reminded of the haunted feeling I had when I first came here and learned of its history.

We're led into a larger brightly lit room despite the lack of windows. The floor is covered in squishy black padding. Ryne stands at the front of the room, with the five eligible betas along the walls, but it's not just them. There are around twenty or so other wolves as well. They all stand on the edges of the padding. We huddle in a circle in the middle. The Madames go and stand among the wolves.

I want to whisper to Joanna about what is going on, but then I remember what Madame Delphine said, and I can't afford to lose any points.

Ryne leans against a bench and stares at us with crossed arms. His gaze lingers on mine for a few seconds longer than everyone else's, and he nods once, as if he's trying to tell me something. I'm completely captivated by him, and my stomach burns with that thought.

Someone hits me from the side, and another pair of forceful hands shove me to the ground. A boot kicks my ribs, and I curl into a ball as fists pummel me. I'm in shock. What is going on? What do I do?

"Help," I scream out. "Please!" I cover my head, but I'm still being hit and kicked from all sides. Through the flurry of arms and legs, I spot the rest of the wolves holding the other girls back. "Help," I scream once again.

"Fight back," a fierce voice whispers in my ear. It's Grady. His familiar voice is all it takes. I kick out, and my foot connects with a shin. Then I send my arms flailing, scratching and clawing anything I can reach. An elbow slams into my mouth, and I taste blood.

And then I'm alone, lying on the ground, breathing hard. Anders, Grady, and Nico retreat.

Ryne stands over me and holds out a hand. I take it, allowing him to hoist me up. He leans down low. "Are you okay?" he asks.

I take stock of my body. In spite of the pummeling, nothing hurts but my shoulder where I hit the ground and my mouth where I bit my lip when Anders's stupid elbow hit me. "Yes."

"Then come with me."

He takes my hand and leads me to the front of the room. My breathing is still rapid, and my heart races, but other than that, I'm fine and refuse to show weakness.

The rest of the wolves are positioning the girls around the room so they are all spread out. Joanna struggles against Grady's grip, but I'll be honest that she doesn't seem to be resisting his touch as much as she's enjoying it, and he's definitely smirking.

Ryne drops my hand and addresses the girls.

"Who can tell me what changed? Why did they stop beating on her?"

Joanna thrusts her hand up in the air, her expression fierce.

"Joanna?" Ryne calls on her.

"She kicked Anders."

"That's right. She started to fight back. As you can see, she is fine. While it looked like she was getting beat up, my wolves were careful not to hurt her. Today we not only have the betas who are your potential mates but also several others." I look around at the men I don't recognize. I count fifteen who've been added to our usual group. "Some are already mated," he continues, "and others have not yet decided to take a mate. They will assist with your training today. Five of you will be lucky enough to become a beta wife. That means that you will bear our children and raise them in your own homes. You must learn how to protect not only yourselves but also your children in case we are not around. Our wives must be warriors as well as ladies."

"Oh, is that all?" Joanna tuts.

I'm sure she's going to get points deducted right here on the spot, but Ryne simply ignores her. "Today, you begin your combat training. We will return once a week to work with you, but most of the time it will just be the five of us, so take advantage of the help we have today and soak in everything we teach you."

I stand a little taller, assessing the group of men for who I think will be the hardest to beat.

"Now, the reason we attacked Poppy first was

because she wasn't paying attention to her surroundings. Let that be your first lesson."

Not paying attention? I was distracted by *him*. Fury burns in my chest. I hate him.

"Poppy, you may rejoin the others."

I wipe blood from my mouth and glare at the infuriating man as I take the empty space between Charlotte and Faye. I want to go stand by Joanna, but she's too far back, and if I were to trek back there, I would draw too much attention to myself. The last thing I want is to get blindsided by these brutes again.

Ryne continues to address us. "Today is a test of endurance. You fight until you drop. The last one standing gets top points for the day. You are allowed to fight back as fiercely as you wish." He smiles. "My advice? Pace yourself, but don't hold anything back either."

Sounds like a contradiction to me.

Not a moment passes before the wolves are on us, shoving and hitting. Anders has come after me, singling me out as he often does, and I fight him with every ounce of energy I have. None of his blows cause me much pain, but he's relentless. I want to hurt him, to punish him for what he did to Willow, but I'm no good at this. Time passes, but I don't even know how long. Ryne walks among us, observing, sometimes calling out instructions, but never touches anyone.

Faye is the first to fall and not get back up. I don't see

much, but the next time I catch a glimpse of her, she is sitting along the wall, sipping out of a bottle of water with an apple in her hand, scowling at the rest of us.

My arms tire, and most of my blows don't seem to faze Anders, so I use my foot to kick out, and he doubles over. He glares at me and lashes out, his fist connecting with my face. My head snaps back, and stars blur in my eyes. When my vision clears, Ryne is standing between me and Anders. "We don't hurt them," he hisses. "I thought that was clear."

Anders gives a nod. Ryne turns around. "Are you okay? Maybe you should go sit down."

I shake my head. Half the girls are already out, and I'm not ready to join them. "I'm fine."

He purses his lips. "As you wish. Anders, you walk around and see how everyone is doing. I'll continue here with Poppy."

Anders chuckles to himself but leaves, and Ryne spins, hitting me across the ribs. His blows are softer than Anders had been, more controlled, but he's faster, and I find myself tiring quickly from the constant defense. Our eyes lock as we fight, and something powerful yet beautiful ignites within me, like a lightning strike connecting with sand, transforming it to glass. I'm focused on Ryne's every movement, blocking as often as I can. My muscles beg for rest, but I use it as fuel to keep going. I won't give up.

I don't know how long the fight continues before

Ryne steps back, his hands up. "It's over."

I shake my head. "No. I can keep going."

He chuckles, and pride lights his eyes. "Everyone else is on the floor and has been for the last ten minutes. You are the last one standing. Good job."

Madame Lucille brings me a bottle of water and a banana. I remain standing, not wanting to look weak, but my legs shake.

Ryne doesn't move far from me as he addresses the group. "I need you all up and facing your opponents once again." There is a collective groan, but the wolves help the girls up. Once everyone is back on their feet, Ryne continues. "While you may see us as your enemy today, we are not. We care deeply for your welfare. Every week we will fight, and then you will leave with a hug to remind you that we are not your enemy."

Could've fooled me.

Ryne pulls me close. He smells of man and wolf, and I'm strangely attracted to that. I wrap my arms around his waist. I don't want to allow myself to relax, to let him think I trust him or care to be here, but it's like a string within me snaps, and my knees go weak. Ryne shifts and just holds me for a moment. Something changes between us in that hug. It's not sexual by any means, but there is a form of affection there. It's strong and comforting. Is it friendship? Respect? I'm not sure, but I melt into it, wanting to stay here with him and forget about everything else.

There's a light tapping on the door, and I look up as Knox steps into the room. Fire flares in my belly. His face is an unreadable mask as he takes us in, our bruises and all, his gaze finally landing on me like a pile of rocks. His eyes flash cold just before he looks down at his shoes.

"What's this slave doing here among our women?" Justin sneers and spits at Knox's feet. Faye beams at the guy like his behavior is to be admired.

Ryne holds up one hand and keeps me tucked against him with the other. "Careful, Justin, this slave has earned a place as my right-hand man, or have you already forgotten the night he defended me before many of my own betas?"

There's a story there. I'm dying to find out what it is. If only I could sneak away with Knox for a few minutes so he could tell me everything. I was hoping we'd get a moment alone in the car yesterday so I could explain myself, but it never happened. He drove Ryne and me back to the house without acknowledging my existence. Ryne didn't let me out of his sight. Even though he didn't stay at Drayton Hall after he dropped me off, it became apparent that human women are not allowed even a second alone with the slave men.

"Prince Ryne, please forgive the interruption." Knox looks up again, his pretty eyes saying so much more than his words alone. "The alpha king is here."

Ryne's arm squeezes me closer.

"Do you know why he came to the city early?"

"No, but he insisted his son come to see him at once."

Ryne nods. "Thank you, Knox. I'll be up shortly."

Knox leaves. The energy in the room has shifted. The betas seem more intense than ever, looking to Ryne for direction. Ryne drops his arm and steps away from me. He squares his shoulders and adopts the same jovial facade he used the night of the claiming ceremony. It's the professional version of himself. I don't know what the real version is, but I suspect it's not this.

"Thank you, ladies, for your hard work today. I'm sure I can speak for my betas when I say we are very pleased." His smile is magnetic, and everyone stares at him, a bit of awe in all of our faces. "I hope we didn't frighten you too much, but it's important that you know how to protect yourselves and your pack. Your scores will be posted after dinner. As a reward, you may have the rest of the day off."

Many of the girls squeal with approval. We haven't had free time since arriving here. Every day it's exercise, chores, lessons, meals, sleep, and repeat. But despite the excitement, there's something unsettling about the suddenly open afternoon. I don't think this was part of the plan. The alpha king's arrival has changed things, and I want to know why.

CHAPTER 14

EVEN THOUGH THE women's sitting room is next to my bedroom, I've barely had a chance to spend any time here until today. I share a big plush armchair with Joanna in the corner. We've got a book between our laps, and I'm trying to concentrate on the adventure story as she quietly reads it aloud. To me, the letters are still a bunch of squiggles, but I can't wait to be able to read these stories for myself one day. Books may be my only escape. But even after a few weeks of reading lessons, I can't read more than a few words. I'm the worst out of all the girls. Though only Joanna can read books fluently at this point.

Well, except for Bailey. That girl picked up reading like a fish to water and has had her nose in a book ever since. I sometimes wonder if she even knows what's going on in the real world, because all she seems to care about is reading. I have to admit, I'm kind of jealous. I'd love to be able to escape into a fantasy world right now. And if I don't make it past the Wolf Moon Festival in January, I'll never have enough time to learn. Maybe I won't get a beta, but I hope to at least get reading down before I go.

On the other side of the room, Faye and the rest of the girls sit around on the couches and gossip mercilessly about the betas. So far, we've had little time to really spend with them, so I don't know why they're going on and on about them, as if they really have anything substantial to say. The betas watch us during our lessons but barely talk to us. Madame Vivien let slip that starting next month, we'll have to go on dates with them. I shudder at that thought. I don't want to spend time alone with any of them, especially Anders.

My mind goes back to this morning and the hug Ryne gave me. He's probably the kindest shifter I've met so far, which is odd considering he's the alpha. It's pretty apparent that he wants me to get claimed by a beta, but I can't figure out why he cares so much. I'm one of twenty women here, one of many who come through Drayton Hall every year. Maybe his mother put him up to it so that I'd stop moping around.

Outside, rain pummels the house, but even that isn't enough to drown out the other girls' incessant chattering. Of course, on the one day we have off, a storm blows in, effectively hiding the sun and locking me inside with a bunch of women who hate me. Madame Delphine sent us up here for some "bonding time," but Joanna is the only one who's shown me a shred of kindness and is the only one I'd like to actually bond with.

"Has anyone been kissed yet?" Faye says extra loud so that Joanna and I can hear the question. A few of the girls had the betas paying closer attention to them, but none as much as Faye. The men all seem to try to steal moments to talk to her. But a kiss? It seems unlikely.

Joanna groans and closes the book. "Okay, Faye." She takes the bait. "Tell us who kissed you so we can get back to our lives because we all know that's what this question is really about."

Faye rolls her eyes. "Well, maybe if you weren't such a stuck-up bitch, Grady would've kissed you by now."

"Who's to say he hasn't?"

He hasn't. Joanna doesn't want him to, and I'm sure she'll avoid him for as long as she can, but the pink in Faye's cheeks is totally worth the lie.

Faye straightens her shoulders and tosses back her shiny auburn hair. It's the kind of red that changes with the light, and right now, it's all dark and sultry and perfect. "How about we play a game, Joanna. If you can guess who kissed me on your first try, then I'll do your chores for a week, and if you can't, then you'll do mine."

Joanna scoffs. "Easy, that would be Justin." He's had his eye on Faye since she arrived, and we saw him pull her into an empty room a few days ago between lessons.

Faye smirks. "Nope. You lose."

"Then who?" Charlotte giggles. "Tell us!"

Faye's eyes land right on mine. "Ryne."

"You're lying," I blurt. I shouldn't react to her—this is exactly what she wants—but I can't keep the anger from flaring. Ryne hasn't touched any of us, nor shown her special attention. I know she's lying. She has to be. It's like she's intentionally trying to goad me, not anyone else. Though maybe it was because I fought with him during our defense class this morning. Maybe she noticed our intimate hug.

She leans back in her chair and puffs up her chest. "Ryne is twenty-three years old, Poppy. He's obviously very experienced with women, and he's here all the time. Why do you think that is?"

"What are you implying?" Joanna cuts in. "That he's here for you? Because I haven't seen him so much as utter a word to you." She sets down the book and stands. "You're jealous."

Faye rolls her eyes and stands as well. She walks right up to Joanna. "What would I have to be jealous about?"

"That Ryne—*the alpha*—is paying extra attention to Poppy."

All the girls turn to look at me, and heat begins to crawl up my neck, coloring my cheeks. Is Ryne paying me extra attention? He did show up when I was out with Madame Delphine, and today he cut Anders off to spar with me. When it was all over, he held me. Everything else can be explained away, but that hug. I shake my head. Everyone got hugs, right? So what if ours felt special? Maybe all the girls felt that way about their hug. There is no way Ryne cares one iota about me. And even if he did, it wouldn't matter. He's the alpha prince, and he's not claiming a wife this year.

Faye is slowly turning the color of a ripe tomato, and I realize Joanna is right. Faye is jealous. It sends a shock of pride right through my center.

"Oh please," Faye sputters. "Ryne's still a young alpha. He's not here for a wife. He's here to make sure his betas get what they need and maybe to get a few of his own needs taken care of. Which *I* can easily take care of for him."

"Oh, and is that a good idea considering you have to keep your virtue intact to land a beta?" I shouldn't continue to goad her, but I can't help myself.

"You're going to get yourself kicked out of here, and it'll be your own fault."

Faye rolls her eyes. "Ryne has the mating house for *that,* but it doesn't mean he can't get a taste of his favorite claimed girls every once in a while." Faye grins wickedly. "Why do you think he kissed me? Because he knows I will keep things interesting. Poppy isn't pretty enough to get anyone's attention. Ryne just talks to her because she fights like a man." She glares down at me, and I can't take it. I get up and join Joanna.

Now that I'm standing, I'm able to look down my nose at Faye, and I'll admit it feels good. I ignore the comment about me not being pretty because I know she's right. I'm plainer than all the other girls and don't have the same curves they do, but so what? Charlotte and the other girls giggle. This is the best entertainment they've had in a long time.

"So does Ryne kiss you, Poppy?" Faye presses, batting her long dark eyelashes to taunt me. "Does he corner you behind the willow tree and run his hands all over you and kiss you like you are the only woman in the world, or is that just me?"

Heat burns me up. I'm embarrassed and angry, confused and defeated, and I'm just standing here like an idiot. What can I say? Nothing. I shouldn't even care that she's making out with Ryne. He's of no consequence to me.

Faye smirks. "That's what I thought. You don't even belong here. I heard what happened to your sister. I guess I shouldn't be surprised that she turned out to be even more pathetic with men than you are." She turns, her long shiny hair flipping.

I can handle rude comments about myself all day long, but I won't stand for insults about my sister. Red pulses through me, and I grab hold of Faye's stupid hair and pull. She screams as I twist her toward me, yanking harder. She reaches for me, but I dodge her, so instead of my face, her hands grip my wrists, nails clawing. I hiss and release her.

"What is wrong with you?" she screeches and dives for me. I catch her against my stomach and wrench my knee up into her ribcage. She growls and bites my arm—actually bites me! I scream and push her away, but only so I can get her in the position I need to swipe at her face and draw blood.

Hands grab hold of my upper arms, pulling me back. Joanna.

"Stop!" Madame Delphine yells as she and Madame Vivien burst into the room. "What's going on here?"

"Poppy attacked Faye," Charlotte explains, and the other girls nod vigorously. I give Charlotte the nastiest glare possible. *Traitor.*

Madame Delphine turns on me. "Is this true, child?"

"She provoked me."

"No, I didn't!" Faye insists, standing and brushing herself off. Crocodile tears shine in her eyes, and blood drips down her cheek. "We were just talking about the men, and she blindsided me."

"That's not how it happened," Joanna interjects. She drops her hands and stands in front of me like a protector. It's something Willow would do.

"Yes, it is." Charlotte gasps, and my glare deepens. "What is wrong with you two? You've banded together to hate the rest of us from day one."

"They think Grady will persuade one of his buddies to choose Poppy," says one of the girls who I've never even talked to. She speaks like she's the authority on friendship with Joanna. Her name's Ivy, and she came here from the distillery village, so it's no surprise that she's backing up her friend. I feel like I should tell Madame Delphine Faye's comment about Willow, but the words stick in my throat.

"I think I've heard enough." Madame Delphine sighs and levels me with an exasperated look. "Violence toward your fellow claimed is strictly prohibited. I don't care if Faye provoked you. You cannot start fights. You had managed to get out of last place today, Poppy. You were the top girl this morning. And now look at what you've done. I have no choice but to deduct points."

I'm so angry that I don't even care about the stupid leaderboard right now. "This is what Faye wanted." I point at her. "You couldn't stand that you placed last at combat today and that I won."

Faye is always at the top of the board, but today, she dropped down three places because she can't fight to save her life. Joanna snagged the top spot. She seems to be good at everything. And I jumped up from the twentieth spot to the sixth. So much for that lasting.

"You're crazy!" Faye has the audacity to look totally shocked and a little bit afraid.

I smile at the angry red scratches marring her otherwise perfect face, hoping they leave a scar. She deserves to be as ugly on the outside as she is on the inside. "Stay away from me, and never say another word about my sister."

I storm to my bedroom, slamming the door behind me so hard that the walls rattle. I can still hear when Faye yells after me that I'm a delusional freak who will never land a beta.

She's right. I know she's right. This argument isn't even about Ryne because he's not interested, and anyway, he angers me every other time we interact. This is about fighting for a life that isn't complete hell. It's what Willow would want me to do. I'll never forget what I saw yesterday at the mating house, and I'm not going to give up on my future. Nor am I going to let Faye win. Not again.

CHAPTER 15

ON FRIDAYS, whoever is at the top of the leaderboard gets the afternoon off, and today that happens to be Joanna. The rest of us are usually assigned extra study in whatever subject is our weakest. For me, that's everything except for combat and exercise, and I normally find myself alone with Madame Vivien or Madame Lucille, working on art or reading or my worst nightmare—singing.

After lunch one Friday in late October, Madame Delphine asks me and Joanna to stay behind as the girls head off to their extra lessons. I wonder if we're in trouble.

"Grady has requested this afternoon to take you out, Joanna."

Joanna crosses her arms and glowers at Madame

Delphine. "I was at the top today. That means I get to choose what I do this afternoon."

"Actually, it doesn't. It just means that you don't have to do extra lessons. He will be here in twenty minutes to pick you up. He also requested that Poppy accompany you. I think perhaps he thought you'd be more willing that way."

Joanna considers it for a moment, and I hope she'll say yes. I don't want to do extra lessons, and I like the thought of getting out of the house. Maybe we'll have fun.

"Okay, but only because Poppy is coming with."

"Very well. Madame Lucille has laid out appropriate clothes for your outing. And, Joanna, perhaps you could help Poppy with her hair and makeup."

Joanna nods vigorously and drags me up the stairs. Our gowns brush against each other, and she loops her arm through mine, whispering excitedly. "You know what this means, right? It means that he's bringing another beta. Oh, Faye is going to be so jealous that you got the first date. We're not even supposed to have them until next week."

"What? No." Faye and I have kept away from each other, and I have the sinking feeling that if Joanna is right, then Faye's going to lose her mind.

"You heard Madame. She wants you to look pretty. You know, I'm not convinced that Ryne wants you like

Faye is obviously worried about, but Madame Delphine seems to have a soft spot for you."

Yeah, and she's Ryne's mother. But I don't think any of the other girls know that. Joanna knows though. The first night here she called Madame Delphine the mother of the most high. I asked her about it later, and she said that because the textile workers sometimes come into the city to do fittings, she learned the truth of this place through the whisperings her mother heard. It's how she knew about what the claiming really meant and why she resisted coming here.

"Was your mother at the claiming?" I frown.

She shakes her head. "I refused to let my parents come. They probably would've got themselves killed. They hate the claiming more than I do."

And my mother pushed me to Anders after he murdered my sister.

Thoughts of that day swirl around in my head as I quickly remove my gown and change into a white tank and tight black pants with tall leather boots. I wonder what would have been different if my people of Northwest knew the truth of our claiming—if my mother had known the truth. Would it have made a difference? I remember the way she gave me away so easily, how she called Anders "my lord," and my chest burns.

Joanna knocks on my door, and I let her in. She's in a matching outfit that looks incredible on her. "We must be doing something active. Otherwise, Lucille would've set us out more stupid dresses. Now sit and let me fix you up."

She puts my plain brown hair back into a fancy braid and puts all kinds of stuff on my face. I've never even worn makeup before, but it makes my eyes look bigger. I've always thought they were a muddy cinnamon color, but right now, they shine like bright amber. I smile to myself and thank her.

"You make a great canvas, Poppy. I only accentuated what's already there."

I don't have anything to say to that. I've never believed I was beautiful. I still don't, but at least I'm presentable now. We manage to make it back downstairs in just under twenty minutes.

Madame Delphine appraises us both. "Good job, Joanna. She looks beautiful."

I flush, knowing it can't possibly be true, but secretly hope the others will think I look semi-decent.

"Thanks," Joanna says, smiling at me. "She *is* beautiful."

"Now. Grady will have you both back here just before dark. It's the full moon, so everyone will be locked up tight, and several betas will guard the house."

I've been dreading this night. Full moons always come with anxiety, but our village never got attacked, so it was easy to pretend nothing would happen. Now that I've seen first-hand what the lycans are capable of, I'm never going to let my guard down during the full moon again.

Outside, Ryne and Grady lean against the shiny black car. When they see us coming down the steps, they stand straight and grin. Joanna groans, and my eyes lock on Ryne. He's staring at me. I hadn't been expecting him. Is he my date? No, that's silly. He's probably dropping Grady off or something. I'm sure one of the betas will be my date. Hopefully not Anders. Maybe Justin, Cade, or Nico. I need to get to know them better.

Knox gets out of the car and stops short when he sees me, the color draining from his face. My heart races, and I wish more than anything that I could save him from this life of servitude.

"Can't have her, man," Grady laughs, patting Knox on the back. "She's mine." They think he's looking at Joanna, but I know the truth.

Knox laughs along and opens the door for us. When Joanna and I climb into the back, he shoots me a pleading look. Grady slides in next to Joanna, and Knox closes us inside. Ryne sits up front. Knox gets behind the wheel, and away we go.

Joanna elbows me in the side and mouths, "Ryne is your date."

I shake my head. It can't be. They're just giving us a ride somewhere. Maybe I don't have a date after all, or maybe one of the other betas is meeting us somewhere. Whatever it is, I'm sure it's not a date. Dating is what people do when they're looking to find the right person for marriage. Ryne doesn't date the claimed. He goes to the mating house and leads his pack and nothing more.

The car ride is thick with tension. Joanna won't talk to Grady, and Knox and Ryne both keep checking the rearview mirror to look at me. I don't know which boy to give my attention to, so I mostly stare out the window and try to keep from blushing. I need to get a good look in a mirror soon because apparently, whatever Joanna did with my hair and makeup is working.

When we arrive at the large barn-like structure and get out of the car, the scent of animals and grass and crisp autumn sunshine sends a wave of happiness through me—happiness and longing for home. Vast fields with horses lie parallel to either side of the dirt drive, and the trees in the distance are sprinkled with reds, yellows, and oranges.

Everything I thought I knew about Ryne clashes with the relaxed man who laces his arm through mine. I guess he's my date after all. I should be disappointed. I should be wanting him to be a beta, but I'm not. A thrill of excitement races through my bloodstream, despite everything I should be feeling. I'm on a date with Ryne. How did this even happen?

"Have you ever ridden horses before?" His voice is playful. I've never seen this side of him.

I shake my head.

"What?" Joanna gushes. "We're riding horses? I've always wanted to!"

"Good, because I'm going to teach you." Grady puts his arm around her shoulders, but she scoffs and pushes him off. She's not angry. She's just being Joanna.

She walks ahead of him into the barn, and he smiles after her like she's the only woman in the world he could ever want, like she's perfect because of her prickliness and not despite it.

"Why me?" I ask before I can stop myself.

"What?" Ryne asks, but he's watching Grady chase after Joanna.

"Why did you ask me to come along?"

His lips twitch. "Maybe I like you."

I snort. "That's absurd."

He stops and stares down at me. "Why is that absurd?"

"I'm hardly pretty like Faye or Charlotte."

Ryne chuckles and continues walking, pulling me along. "It's true that you look nothing like them but trust me when I say that you are very pretty. Just in a different way. Besides, there is often more to desire than just looks, and I happen to enjoy your company more than theirs."

I flush at the compliment. I shouldn't enjoy this, especially since being out here in the fresh air on a farm feels too much like home. We had horses in our village, but I was never allowed to ride them. They were work horses. Maybe today I can just be a girl out with a boy and forget all about the reality of my situation.

Reality can come back tomorrow.

"Thank you," I whisper. My lips twist into a little smile.

He laces his fingers through mine. I can't breathe as we walk the rest of the way in silence, but it's the best feeling.

In the barn, Joanna is bouncing up and down in front of a dark chestnut horse with wide light brown eyes. The coloring of the horse matches her coloring perfectly, like this horse was made for her. Ryne extracts his arm from mine and disappears into a stall. Joanna squeals and drags me closer to the horse.

"Isn't this exciting?" she asks. I've never seen her like this.

"Yeah."

"I've never been this close to a horse before. Do you think it will bite me?"

I chuckle. "No, silly, horses don't bite." At least the ones in our village didn't. I reach my hand up and pat the nose of this one. "See."

Joanna's eyes widen, and she does the same. The horse lets out a snort, and Joanna jumps back, giggling. This is a totally new side to her, and I'm a little in awe.

She loops her arm through mine. "I can't believe it's Ryne out with us. Faye is going to have kittens."

"We aren't telling Faye or anyone else. I don't need another reason for them to attack me."

Joanna's eyes dance. "Fine. We'll keep your little secret. But let's make a deal today. I'll kiss mine if you kiss yours."

"Joanna! No."

Grady returns carrying a large saddle, and Joanna skips away from me, peppering Grady with questions. Who knew that all it would take for Joanna to fall for Grady was a silly horse?

He helps Joanna up into the saddle and then hoists himself up behind her. Joanna is happier than I've ever seen her, and Grady is beaming from ear to ear as he talks her through handling the reins.

"Are you ready?"

I spin and find Ryne next to a black horse with white feet that I swear is twice as tall as the one Grady and Joanna are on.

"That's a big horse," I say. I let out a slow breath and try not to imagine falling off that thing.

Ryne pats the animal's neck. "He is, but he's my favorite. Come on, I'll help you up. He's more docile than Grady's horse."

"Do you ride often?"

"I do. It's peaceful, and it gets me away from the city." He waggles his eyebrows. "My preferred way to roam the outskirts of town is in my wolf. There's really nothing else like it."

"I can only imagine." I remember when he shifted, how natural and powerful he was in that form. But I don't let myself linger on that thought for long.

He places his hands on my waist and easily lifts me up so I can fling my leg over the other side of the horse. I clutch at the saddle; afraid I'm going to fall right off the other side. Ryne climbs up behind me and pulls me close to his firm body. Heat blisters my cheeks. I've never been so close to a man before.

Knox and I were close, and we kissed sometimes, but we mostly held hands and talked. Our bodies never made contact like this. It's both comforting and thrilling all at once.

Ryne kicks the side of the horse, and it starts to walk. I yelp, tightening my grip on the saddle as Ryne chuckles at me. I eventually settle in, allowing myself to enjoy the experience. We spend a while going in circles in the corral, learning the ropes of equine safety. Ryne is a great teacher and comfortable on a horse, even if his body pressing into mine is rather distracting.

"Ready to try something fun?" he asks.

"This *is* fun." I grin. "But sure."

"Hold on." He kicks the horse harder than last time, and the animal begins to gallop. It's not like we're going that fast, but I grip the saddle horn and squeal as adrenaline races through me. Across the corral, Joanna and Grady do the same. Her joyful laugh echoes through the space. We slow, and then Ryne hands me the reins so I can control the horse. It's different when I'm in control. I feel like the horse and I are connected somehow. And when we start to gallop again, it's as if we're about to fly.

We slow, and the stable hand opens a gate to allow us to ride the horses outside into the pasture. The sun is still high in the clear blue sky but will be approaching the horizon soon. By then I'll be safely back at Drayton Hall with the other girls, but I want this moment to last. I want it to be the middle of summer when the sun is generous with her time and not autumn when the nights are long.

"What do you think? Shall we race?" Ryne nods toward Grady and Joanna. She's got the reins, no surprise there, and it's clear that Grady couldn't care less. He's smirking like a love-sick idiot, obviously using this as an opportunity to wrap his arms around her body and get as close as possible. Joanna letting him is a huge step in the right direction for the couple.

I attempt to hand Ryne the reins. "Okay, but you steer the horse."

"Are you sure?"

"You know, for an alpha you sure are quick to hand off control to me."

"Maybe I want to lose control sometimes."

I can't see him, but I can hear the confession in his tone and feel the heat of him against my back. When he takes the reins from me, his hands linger against mine. It sets my belly on fire. How can something that is wrong feel so right? Ryne is a bad person. He's not safe. He isn't even one of the eligible betas. I shouldn't be enjoying his touch.

He calls out to the others, and we're off. I lean down, gripping the saddle, my face close to the horse's mane, and Ryne leans down with me. Our horse is bigger and faster than theirs and shoots out into the lead. Its hooves thunder against the earth, and bits of dirt and grass fly up around us. Cold wind rushes past me, kissing my cheeks. The movement of the animal brings Ryne and me even closer together. It's the most exhilarating moment of my life.

We come to the edge of a wooded area, and Ryne slows us, pumping his fist into the air in victory. He whoops, and I can't help but giggle.

"You won that time," Joanna calls out, "but we'll get you on the way back!"

We ride to a clearing within the trees, and the guys help us off the horses and tie them up. A large, red, checkered blanket is sprawled out in the center with a basket of food and wine sitting on the edge.

"Who's hungry?" Grady announces.

Joanna lights up. "Me! I'm famished."

"Are you hungry?" Ryne asks. I shake my head. I'm really not. We ate lunch before we came, and I'm still wired up from the race. "Me neither. Want to go for a walk?"

I shouldn't want to be alone with him, but I can't

keep myself from nodding. He takes my hand, intertwining his fingers with mine, and leads me farther into the forest.

Fall is in full swing, and I pick up a red leaf that has fallen to the ground. Ryne clears his throat. "Did you spend a lot of time outdoors before you moved here?"

I nearly snort at the idea that I just moved here like I had a choice, but I answer his question anyway. "Yeah. Our homes were small and cramped, and we don't have electricity, but I'm sure you already know that. We all liked being outside, but I guess myself more than others. I enjoyed working in the fields and climbing trees."

Ryne pats the trunk of an old oak. "You mean like this one?"

I gaze up. The nearest limb is five feet off the ground, but I could probably swing myself up onto it.

"Yeah, like that one."

"Come here," he says, pulling me closer to him. He places his wide hands on my sides, just above my hips.

"What are you doing?" I ask.

"Helping you up." He hoists me high into the air, and my squeal nearly drowns out his chuckle. I grab the limb and swing myself up onto it, much like I did on the horse. Then I find the branch above it and pull myself up even farther. Ryne is close behind me as I make my way up the tree. I finally reach a wide limb and sit, my back to the trunk.

Ryne is close behind and sits across from me, straddling the limb. His eyes dance as he studies me. "That was fun. We'll have to climb trees more often."

"My sister, Willow, and I spent a lot of time up in the trees." My voice cracks a little at her name.

Ryne shimmies forward and brushes the hair out of my eyes. My skin burns where his fingers touch. "I am sorry about your sister. Anders's temper gets the best of him. If I had been there, she'd still be alive."

I nod, not wanting to think of that awful moment again. But I can't help the tear that slides down my cheek.

Ryne scoots even closer and brushes it away. "Hey, don't cry. I'm sorry. I didn't mean to make you upset. Tell me more about what your plans had been before coming here."

I pause, because it's not something I'd thought of often at home. In the months leading up to the claiming, I'd been solely focused on Willow leaving me. But I had come of age as well.

"I suppose I would've found a husband and continued working the fields like everyone else. But I also probably would've grown my own garden and helped increase our food supply. I liked working with my mother in hers, but she never had enough time to expand it."

"Why not?"

"Her own duties and general housekeeping. Plus us kids kept her on her toes. I have a little brother too, by the way. My mother's life probably would've been my fate as well."

He's quiet, and I wonder what he thinks of my past. But I don't ask.

The wind rustles the nearby poplar leaves like wind chimes, but I can scarcely focus on that when Ryne's pretty blue eyes stare into mine. This close, I can see the dark rims and the flecks of white. His black hair is tied back today, accentuating sharp cheekbones. There's something so manly about him, so foreign and alluring. Our eyes lock together, and my mind blanks.

He dips his head, moments away from kissing me.

I push my hand against his chest. "Stop."

"What's wrong?" His eyes go cold, and he scoots back. The moment is ruined. I don't understand what he is doing with me.

"What are your intentions?" I blurt.

"Umm—" He scratches the back of his head. "To kiss you."

He says it so plainly, and my stomach lurches.

I summon the courage to tell him exactly what's been on my mind since he slid into the car with us. He's toying with me. "Ryne, if you kiss me, and this becomes a thing between us, then what happens when we get back to the manor? Will your betas still think of me as an option, or will they consider me taken? I know I'm not as desirable as the other girls, but I have to at least try to escape the mating house. Isn't that why you took me there in the first place? To show me what my fate would be if I don't get a beta."

He's quiet for a minute, considering my words carefully. "My betas know I'm not taking a wife anytime soon. This won't matter. In fact, a relationship with me might even make you more desirable to them. It's an honor."

That fire in my belly from before turns to smoke. "The keyword there being might. Have you dated one of the claimed girls before?" I hate to ask the question because the answer might hurt, but I feel like I have a right to know. Willow would be proud. I'm a little surprised at myself as well.

A hard mask passes over his features. "You're right. Let's go back."

We don't talk after that, and I take his non-answer for a yes. He's the alpha, after all. He can take whatever woman he wants just as easily as he can discard her. And what if he takes her virtue also? Does that mean she's ineligible to marry a beta? He won't speak of past relationships with claimed girls, which probably means that whatever happened to them was not a happy ending. If every girl he dated ended up with a beta, then he wouldn't have backed off since that was my whole argument.

But truth be told, it is more than that. I don't want to date him and won't be okay when he gets bored. I have no idea why I caught his eye, and it doesn't matter. What matters is landing a beta so I can still have that family and garden and a semblance of a normal life.

"I think I'm hungry now," I say in a soft voice.

We scramble down the tree, and he helps me out of it but quickly drops his hands from my waist. We walk back to the clearing in a rather awkward silence, only to find Joanna and Grady kissing. Grady holds her like she's the most important thing in his entire world, and I'm faced with the stark truth. They're fated. We're not. Grady will never ever do to Joanna what Ryne is willing to do to me.

He just wants to kiss me and then hand me off to someone else. I don't want that. Even if he could promise that I'd end up with a beta after dating him, I don't think I'd do it. I have more than my body to guard. I have my heart as well.

CHAPTER 16

"YOU WILL BE SLEEPING DOWNSTAIRS TONIGHT," Madame Delphine announces during dinner. We're seated at the dining tables with a bigger feast than normal and immediately cease chattering at her announcement. "Now, girls, I know this may seem a little extreme, but I assure you it is a customary precaution for all humans living in the city to spend full moons under lock and key. The only exceptions are the celebratory moons, but even with those, most humans choose to stay inside." I exchange a worried glance with Joanna, and she grimaces. This doesn't sound good. We were never this locked up in our village. It seems strange that we're in more danger here in the wolf city than we were there.

"It is much easier for us to lock up one or two rooms than to try to board up the entire manor," Delphine continues. "God forbid a lycan got past our border patrols and came here. They would kill you without hesitation."

My stomach goes hard, and I put down my dinner roll. Since the moment Joanna and I were dropped off late this afternoon from our double date, I could think of little else, but now visions of bloodthirsty lycans take over my mind. I'm sure I'll have nightmares tonight, and it's not something I'm looking forward to.

"So chop-chop." Madame Delphine claps her hands. "Finish up and then go get into your pajamas and meet us downstairs."

Charlotte is the first to leave, dashing up the stairs to our bedroom. By the time I go up myself, she's already changed into silky pink pants and a matching button-up. She leans across the vanity with her face inches away from the mirror, staring intently into her eyes. Her cheeks are bright pink as if she's just returned from a run. Sweat beads along her hairline.

"Are you okay?"

She jumps and turns on me with accusatory eyes. Maybe she's getting sick and doesn't want to be left out of the safest spot in the house tonight, but having us all sleep in the same room might not be a good idea.

"I'm fine," she snaps. "Mind your own business." And then she storms away like I've offended her.

"I'll mind my own business when you mind yours," I growl to nobody as I get dressed and head downstairs.

Maybe Charlotte isn't sick. Maybe she's angry about my date with Ryne. I'd hoped to keep it a secret, but that seems to be impossible around here. The second we returned this afternoon, everyone already knew. Their distrustful and jealous faces said it all. I decide to let the Charlotte thing go for now, but I'm going to avoid sleeping next to her just in case she's ill or up to something.

I glance at the board on the way down. My name is third from the bottom. It's not the best position to be in, but at least I've moved up a couple of places.

In the windowless battle room, twenty-three cots are set up, each piled with a fluffy white blanket and pillow. The room's big enough to fit us all plus Madames Delphine, Vivien, and Lucille.

"The rest of the staff left for their own homes hours ago," Madame Delphine says once everyone has arrived. "We will all be staying in here. If you need to use the restroom, one of us can escort you, but please, I'd rather not open this door once it's locked, so I hope you've emptied your bladders already."

A couple of the girls raise their hands sheepishly, and Madame Lucille ushers them out. Everyone seems nervous with their worried eyes and thin lips. Even Faye and Joanna, opposite sides of the same tough-girl coin, are a bit jumpy tonight. The girls from the bathroom run are quick to return, and then we all settle into our beds. Madame Delphine lights a small lamp and turns off the overhead lights before locking us in. She doesn't use a key. She slides a metal barricade across the door that slams shut with a bang.

A few of the girls gasp.

"This is all customary," she assures us. "Lycans rarely make it into the city, but we're being extra careful, especially after the harvest moon last month. Not only are there wolves stationed all over the city and at the borders to the wilds, but your betas are outside, prowling the grounds at this very moment. They'll be out there all night in their wolf forms."

As if on cue, a series of howls echoes outside. Inside, some of the girls start to cry.

"That's our men, isn't it? Not the lycans?" Faye speaks up.

"Yes," Delphine says. "Lycanthrope calls are less . . . organized. They sound more like guttural screeching than actual wolves. And they're much, much louder. Not to worry. Again, this is all normal. Please, let's all try to relax. You're welcome to talk among yourselves for a half-hour, and then it'll be lights out for everyone."

I turn in my bed, ignoring the cot's squeaking, and face Joanna. "Are you scared?"

"No," she whispers. "If anything, I think this would be the perfect time to escape."

"Are you crazy? There are wolves everywhere. And lycans in the wilds. Besides, I thought you liked Grady."

I whisper even lower. "Ryne and I totally saw you two kissing."

She scrunches her cheeks and sighs dreamily. "He is rather nice, isn't he? Better than I thought . . . But he's still not my plan."

"So then what's the real plan here, Joanna? I still don't understand it. Where do you think you'll go?"

"I can't reveal anything yet, but I'm working on it. Besides, we have eleven more months until the claiming. Give me time."

If anyone can find a way out of here, it's Joanna, but that only makes me afraid for her. For as much as that woman is determined, the wolves are too, and they have fangs and claws. Part of me wants to go with her when she escapes, but another part is stuck in the fear of the unknown, and that part might keep me planted right here.

"So what happened with Ryne?" Joanna whispers back. I close my eyes for a second and try to figure out how to respond.

"He tried to kiss me, but I didn't let him."

Her eyes widen. "Why not? He's gorgeous and the alpha. He could help you."

I disagree, but even if she's right, it still doesn't change the fact that I don't want to be used, especially not by someone who could break my heart on a whim.

"Okay, ladies, lights out." Madame Delphine turns off the lamp, plunging the basement into blackness. A few of the girls squeal and giggle. Joanna reaches over and grips my hand. I squeeze back.

"Now, calm down. It would be good for you all to try to get to sleep before the howling of the lycans starts. It'll be much harder then."

The howling of the lycans? We rarely heard their howling back home. This city must be their target, so maybe that explains why they don't come around the villages anymore. But if they're smart enough to have a target, then are they as unhinged as we've been led to believe? If lycans only want human flesh, why go after the wolf shifters at all?

A hush falls across the room, and I replay my afternoon with Ryne again even though I know I shouldn't— the more I push them away, the more the memories flood me. Maybe I should've let him kiss me. He was nice, and his very touch caused my heart to race in a way I've never experienced before. Why did I deny him? I know there were many logical reasons, but here in the dark, I can't think of them.

A howl pierces the silence. It's guttural and screechy, sending warning prickles across my skin. I clamp my hands over my ears.

The howl didn't come from outside.

CHAPTER 17

A CLATTER FOLLOWED by a scream comes from the other side of the room. I spring from my cot and find Joanna's hand. "What's going on?" she asks. It's pitch black. We can't see anything.

"I have no idea," I shout over the noise. Girls are screaming. At first they sound surprised, then frightened, but it's the horrified wails of pain that will forever be etched into my memory. Joanna and I move away from the noise and run into other girls doing the same. Something loud and metallic sounding slams against a wall.

"Don't step on me," Faye's voice growls, and she shoves me hard.

The lamp light flicks on, momentarily blinding me. I squint to let my eyes adjust.

Then I scramble back. A fully grown lycan towers

over Madame Lucille. It's so tall that its head brushes the ceiling. Its grotesque limbs are covered in matted gray hair, and saliva drips from its snarling mouth.

Madame Lucille holds up her hands. "No, no, no," she gasps. The lycan bares long bloody teeth, snapping them shut around Madame Lucille's neck. Blood spurts around the monster's mouth as it gives a mighty shake. Madame Lucille's body goes flying one direction and her head another, an arc of blood between them.

More screams.

The lycan crouches onto all fours and turns on us, surveying the room with bloodthirsty eyes. They shine like the pale white of the moon. We're all dead.

Madame Delphine scrambles at the door, fumbling with the lock. Time seems to slow as she flings it up and pushes the door wide. A gust of wind blows into the room, and the lycan stands up on its haunches and sniffs. Madame Delphine swings around to hold the door open from behind, and we all will it to run out.

It doesn't.

It takes a slow walk around the room. None of us move. The lycan sniffs at Faye, its muzzle grazing her auburn hair, and a trickle of urine slides down her leg. I'd do the same if I were in her shoes. Joanna and I are pressed up against the wall, but the creature is so close that we can smell its putrid breath. It moves even closer to Faye, its mouth slowly opening. It's going to bite her.

I don't think. I just react. "Hey!" I yell. "Over here!"

It turns its head, eyes narrowing in on me. Oh no, what have I done?

I let go of Joanna and inch along the wall toward the door. I keep my eyes locked on the lycan as it stalks toward me. I need a weapon. Something. Anything. But there's nothing. We're trapped in here with this monster and now it's picked me as its next victim. It lowers onto its haunches, readying to pounce. Fear twists my stomach, and I think I might vomit. I can't let it touch me. I won't die tonight.

It dives for me, but I roll out of the way at the last second. Its long claws decimate the floor right where I was standing moments before. Adrenaline urges me to keep moving. If I can just get out the door, maybe I can find something to fight it with. This is our sparring room, but there are no weapons in here. We were told we'd be learning weapons training later, but I can see now that to have us wait was completely foolish. We're not going to be fighting hand-to-hand combat against *lycan*. If only there were something here. I'm suddenly on my hands and knees, crawling as fast as I can for the exit, but there's no way I can outrun the monster.

Another lycan howls from outside the house. Ours jerks its head around and lets out its own higher-pitched howl. My ears ring, and the monster turns back again, coming right for me. I scream, sure this is going to be the end. I hope my death is quick. I know it won't be painless. I ready myself to fight to the bitter end, but it passes me, taking off out the door.

Madame Delphine slumps against it.

"What are you doing?" Madame Vivien hisses at her. "Shut the door."

Footsteps pound down the stairs, and six wolves race into the room. The girls are yelling to close the door. Madame Delphine slams the door shut and locks all of us inside. The room is a mess. There's blood everywhere and a tangle of bodies on the far side. Joanna appears next to me and wraps her arms around my neck. "Are you okay? Did it bite you?"

Before I can answer, the wolves shift into men—our betas and Ryne—and I avert my eyes at their nakedness. Grady races over to us and jerks Joanna away from me. He hugs her tight, and she squirms in his arms. "Let me go."

He obliges, but he keeps her close. "Are you hurt?"

She keeps her eyes planted firmly on his face. "I'm fine. Now would you go put some clothes on?"

The other wolves are with Madame Delphine by a chest of drawers. She hands them all loose black shorts for them to dress into, though I don't think they care. Grady drags Joanna with him to the others and gets himself a pair.

Ryne meets my eye but doesn't come over to me, and I don't move either. He's covered in dirt and blood, anger contorting his handsome face into something unrecognizable. He puts a hand on his mother's shoulder and whispers something in her ear. She whimpers, a tear streaking down her cheek, and nods. She whispers something back to him, and he looks at me for a long moment.

Ryne speaks to his betas loud enough for us to hear, even over the sound of all the girls crying. I'm one of them—I can't help it. I've never seen so much blood, and now that it's over, the reality of it hits me square in the chest. "Anders, inspect everyone for bites. Nico and Justin, take the bodies away and burn them."

I blink at that word, bodies.

Plural.

I don't want to look, don't want to know who else the lycan has killed.

Ryne turns to Grady and Cade. "We're going after her."

"Who?" the question slips from my tongue.

Ryne levels me with a sullen expression. "Charlotte."

I gasp, and my thoughts quickly fill with shame. I should have known. I spent the last month in the same room as her. How did I not see it before? *She was bit!* That night at the Wolf Moon Festival, she was bit . . .

And she didn't want anyone to know, least of all her roommate.

Grady gives Joanna a quick hug but ultimately does as his alpha instructs, sprinting out of the room. Cade and Ryne follow. Nico and Justin begin carrying the bodies out and I can't help but look this time. The two girls who had been sleeping on the other side of Charlotte have been shredded to bloody pieces. They're in worse shape than Madame Lucille even, and she's been decapitated.

Now that I'm looking, I can't stop staring.

Someone tugs on my arm, and I turn to Faye, who swings her hand, slapping me clean across the face. I screech and fall to my butt. "She's from *your* village! She was *your* roommate. Why did you protect her?"

I shake my head. "I—I didn't know." But I should have. She wouldn't change her clothing in front of me. She was cagey and withdrawn. She was meaner than I've ever known her to be, and she even looked sick tonight. How did I not see it?

"Faye, you should be grateful for Poppy. She saved your ass tonight," Joanna cuts in. She storms across the room and comes to stand between me and Faye.

"Not when it was her fault to begin with!" Faye snarls back.

She's right. The signs were there.

Faye lunges forward past Joanna to get to me, but Joanna catches her, and the two start clawing at each other. Madame Delphine is quick to pull them apart. "Enough. We'll make inquiries later. Right now we have to inspect everyone for bites. There's no time to waste."

"That's right." Anders strides to the middle of the room. "Everybody strip."

"Excuse me?" Joanna barks. "I'm not stripping for anyone."

Anders narrows his icy eyes. His bronzed skin is covered in sweat, and the lines around his eyes and mouth are deeper than normal. He's not playing around. "If you don't let me inspect you for bites, then I will assume you are infected, and I will kill you myself."

"But Grady—"

"Grady isn't here," he roars. "And this is a command from the alpha, so Grady wouldn't be able to stop me."

Joanna looks to Madame Delphine, who nods in confirmation.

Anders laughs and opens his hands wide. I think his expression is an attempt at being charming, but I find it severely lacking.

"If anyone needs help removing their clothing, that can be arranged," he jokes.

Nobody laughs.

We do as we're told. I'm shaking, embarrassed, and hating my lack of curves even more now that I have to undress in front of other girls who've spent the last month belittling me. But maybe we'll all be too traumatized by what happened tonight to remember much of this come morning. No. It will be an extra dark stain on our time here at Drayton Hall, one we'll want to forget, but I'm sure we won't.

Cool air wraps around my limbs as I stand naked, one hand over each of my private areas. Anders takes his time inspecting every inch of the girls. He takes extra time with Joanna just to make her mad, and of course it works. Her cheeks flame, but she stands tall, refusing to back down. He tugs at her short hair, and she snaps her head back. He shakes his head and moves on. When he gets to me, our eyes lock. Even though his are hooded in shadow and almost impossible to read, the lust swirling with them is unmistakable.

"Drop your hands," he says slowly.

I swallow hard and release them from where they're covering me. What I don't expect is his touch. I flinch away. "You didn't touch the other girls," I breathe.

"Don't move," he says slowly. "And don't talk either. I like you better when you don't talk." And then he runs his sweaty hands across my torso and around to my lower back, his fingers edging along the top of my cheeks. My stomach churns. All he would have to do is move them a few inches lower to cup my butt and it would be the exact same move he did to Willow. I should fight back as she did, but before I can channel my dead sister's bravery, his hands are gone, and he steps away to inspect the next girl. Humiliated, I turn away and hurry back into my pajamas.

"Please, don't," the girl whimpers.

I swing around to watch, assuming he's doing the same to her as he just did to me, but I'm wrong.

A wolfish growl rips through the room as he picks her up, naked and all, carrying her away. "She's been bitten," he calls to us. "I'll be back in five minutes. Don't move."

"What's he going to do to her?" Ivy asks.

Faye snorts bitterly. "Kill her and burn her. Same as they do to any human who's been bit."

Joanna makes for the door. "Not on my watch. It's not her fault."

Madame Delphine and Madame Vivien block her path.

"Move out of my way!"

"Get back in line, Joanna." Madame Delphine sounds bone tired. "There's nothing anyone can do. He'll make it quick and as painless as possible." Her sad eyes travel across the lot of us. "And then he'll finish his inspection on the rest of you."

"Has anyone else been bitten?" Madame Vivien asks gently. Her face is streaked with tears. I've never seen her like this. She's normally such a professional woman. As an instructor and house mother, she has a quiet and stern way about her. "It would be better if you told us now," she continues. "We should have inspected you after the lycanthropes attack at the harvest moon festival. We made a grave mistake that has cost us five lives." Tears brim in her eyes.

First to go were Teresa and Lily, but at least they were murdered in darkness, where we didn't have to watch it happen. But I'll never forget the way Madame Lucille died so similarly to Willow. And now Belinda has gone with Anders to die. I hope they're right, and that he'll make it quick, but I have my doubts.

"Who's the fifth life?" someone asks.

"Charlotte, of course." Madame Delphine sighs regretfully. "They'll hunt her down and kill her. But even if she somehow manages to get away and can find a way to survive in the wilds, she's lost to the lycanthropic virus. Charlotte as you knew her is gone."

I plop down on the cot and bury my face in my palms. It's no secret that I never particularly liked Charlotte, but she didn't deserve this. She should have told someone about the bite. But then what would have happened? She'd have been sentenced to death, no questions asked, no way to plead her case. Nothing. She was probably scared out of her mind all month long. Maybe if I'd been a better friend to her, she would have confessed the bite to me, and I could have somehow helped her. None of these people had to die. All of this could've been avoided.

Faye was right to slap me.

Anders strolls back into the room and zeros in on the girls who haven't dressed yet. "Who's next?"

CHAPTER 18

AFTER IT'S OVER, we're sent back to our bedrooms, and more betas are called in to stand guard at our doors. Joanna and I lie there in the dark, neither one of us able to speak. She took Charlotte's bed because she didn't want me to be alone. The memories of tonight scrape through my mind like the edge of a knife, and I don't think I'll be able to sleep. I can't help but stare at the darkened window. I'm not safe in here either, but I don't have anywhere else to go.

Sometime later there's knocking on the door, and I'm jolted awake. Sunlight filters through the curtains, just like any other morning.

"No workouts today." I hear Madame Vivien through the door. "Get dressed in your gowns and come down for breakfast."

Joanna has altered all my outfits by now, and the ones that we weren't able to make use of, Madame Delphine switched out for new ones. I choose my simplest gown. It's black and unadorned with lace or jewels, but it's still tight in the bodice and flares out at the waist. It's uncomfortable, and I'd give anything to swap these gowns out for my ugly work clothes back home. I wonder if I'll ever wear farming clothes again.

"I'm going to wear black too," Joanna says. "We all should." She sits me down and begins brushing my hair out for me. I didn't have to ask. She just knew I needed her help today. "It's not your fault, you know."

"Isn't it?" I let out a breath. I can still smell Charlotte's rosy scent in this room.

"No, it isn't," she insists. "It's the wolves, and it's the lycans, and *Charlotte's*. And I'm not going to let anyone blame you for it, not even you."

I reach out and pat her hand, holding her gaze in the mirror. Her brown eyes hold mine and I find strength there, as if she's giving it to me from sheer force of will. I've never had a friend like her—someone who feels like blood even though they aren't. "Thank you."

Joanna finishes up and then leaves to get herself dressed. As she goes, I notice little brown specks of dried blood on the back of her silk pajamas. I don't think anyone got out of that room without some kind of stain, visible or otherwise.

Breakfast is a solemn affair. Most of us can't even

eat. When the perimeter is declared to be safe, we're sent outside to an art lesson. I sit and stare at the white canvas but don't touch a single drop of paint. The betas don't join us, and nobody speaks to me.

That night at dinner, Faye asks Madame Delphine the question we're all wondering. "Excuse me, Madame," she says, between sips of water. "Did they ever find Charlotte?"

"Not yet," Madame Delphine replies. "They lost her scent at the river. She's probably to the wilds by now."

I wonder what she's feeling. Is she afraid? Angry? Regretful? Does she even remember what she did to us? Did she know she was going to turn? Maybe she thought she wasn't infected. Maybe she did, and she wanted to hurt us. I'll never know the answers to these questions.

The next morning it's back to business as usual. We meet out on the lawn. Madame Vivien is there to give us our workout assignment.

"Poppy," she calls to me. There's a darkness in her eyes—something I've never seen there before. "Come here."

I go to her, and she glares down at me. She's one of the only women I've met who's actually taller than I am. "You and I are going to be doing a one-on-one workout today." She looks to the others. "Go ahead and do whatever exercises you'd like."

Whispers erupt, and a few head off to run while most stick close by, their eyes never straying too far from me and Madame Vivien. "Do one hundred pushups." She points to the ground. I stare at her for a second. "Now. Go!"

I drop down and start. My muscles are tired, but I endure and go as quickly as I can. I have a feeling this is just the beginning of what's going to be an intense hour. A minute later, someone drops down next to me.

"What are you doing, Joanna?" Madame Vivien asks.

"You said we could do whatever exercise we wanted," Joanna hisses. "So I'm going to stick with my friend and do what she does. If you want to punish her for something she had absolutely no control over, then you can punish me as well."

I can't believe Joanna is calling her out like that. Apparently, Madame Vivien can't either, because she huffs out a breath and stalks away. But she's back as soon as the push ups are done and tells me to get up and do a hundred burpees.

"I don't know what that is."

Her face goes red. "Watch carefully." She drops down, extends her legs back, brings them in again, and stands back up. "Now, go." She smirks at Joanna. "Both of you."

We start, and I quickly realize these are ten times harder because they combine cardio with pushups, and my arms are already screaming. The rest of the hour continues much the same way with a series of difficult exercises, many of them new to me, but I don't mind. Maybe I deserve to be punished, maybe I don't, but I like the way my thoughts go numb. Every muscle screams for relief, but I don't let up. I have to be stronger. And whenever Madame Vivien gives me a new exercise, I treat it like a challenge. Sweat pours from my body, and I gasp for every breath. I need water, but I don't ask. My only regret is that Joanna is doing this with me, but she never once complains.

"What's going on here?" Grady's voice cuts through the cool morning. Joanna and I turn from where we're doing sit-ups with Madame Vivien looming over us like a mountain of rage. He stands with Ryne, and both of them are staring.

"These girls are getting a personal training session from me," Madame Vivien says. "You do not need to concern yourselves with their physical fitness. That's my job."

"It looks like you're trying to hurt them." Grady storms over. He hauls Joanna up and tucks her under his arm. "Do they even have water?"

"I assure you that I know exactly what I'm doing," Madame Vivien snaps.

"Go inside." Ryne steps forward, his eyes leveled on our house mother. "We will finish up with the ladies."

She huffs and stomps off.

"Let's get you something to drink." Grady walks Joanna toward the back of the house where the kitchen door is located. Ryne and I stand there, staring at each other. My breath starts to slow, and now that I've stopped moving, my mind begins to let the troubled thoughts in.

"Why did you do that?" I ask. "I had it under control."

He folds his arms over his broad chest and glowers at me. "I was trying to help you."

"Madame Vivien doesn't need to be ordered around on my behalf. If I'm ever going to get her to respect me, then I have to show her I'm strong."

"The woman lost her best friend of many years," he challenges, "and she was taking it out on the one person she has left to blame."

So he blames me too? A wash of regret prickles through me, and I turn away. He reaches out and snatches my hand. I don't turn back. "Hey, I didn't mean it like that. There's no logic behind blaming you, and I don't, and I'm sorry if others do. If anyone's to blame, it's me. I'm the alpha of this pack. Protecting this manor is my job."

I scoff at that, ripping my hand from his and walking toward the house.

"Why are you angry with me?" he asks.

"I agree that you should protect us, Ryne," I say, flipping back around. I wipe the sweat from my forehead, but not because I care what he thinks of me right now. All my guilt has balled into anger that I want to hurl right at him. "What is the point of our combat training, huh? We fight you guys hand to hand. That does nothing to prepare us for a real attack."

"There's a method—"

"Well then, your method's crap! We should be fighting you in wolf form, in your *strongest* form. And we should be learning to use weapons."

He shakes his head. "These things take time. Once we get through the first two rounds of cuts, we will spend the second half of the year working with weapons. But our men will not turn into wolves to fight you. It's too dangerous."

"Why are we bothering with this becoming-a-proper-lady nonsense when there's a real threat out there? We should do everything I've suggested, and we should do it now."

"No." His word is hard and fast, like a slap to the cheek.

I'm filled with disgust. "Every single woman who comes to the Carolina Pack deserves to learn how to protect herself." My throat goes raw. "Especially the ones who are sent to the mating houses."

His face stills, and his eyes narrow. "You don't trust me."

"No, I don't." And then I turn and run away toward the kitchen. I need to find water and a chance to breathe,

but most of all I need to get away from him before I say
something else I might regret. Because as soon as I
blurted that I didn't trust him, deep down I knew I was
lying. I shouldn't trust him, but for some reason I do, and
I still can't figure out why.

CHAPTER 19

I WAKE UP GASPING. Sweat beads along my hair-line, reminding me of the blood that haunts my dreams every night. I sit up in the dark, clutching my chest. *Another nightmare.* It feels like it's been ages since I slept soundly, and with the next full moon coming up in only a week, I don't know how I'll ever sleep well again. I look over to Charlotte's bed, relieved to find a mound of short dark hair on the white pillow instead of Charlotte's long blonde curls. Joanna moved in to get away from Faye, but also, I suspect, to comfort me. At least I didn't wake her up with this latest nightmare.

The weeks since that terrible full moon have passed by in a blur. They never found Charlotte. I worry that she'll come back for me. It's gotten so bad that every night I end up dreaming about lycan fangs and pooling blood and horrible, horrible screaming. The rest of the girls hate me more than ever. Faye keeps telling them I must have known, and that I was hoping Charlotte would take out my competition. There's no use defending myself because the girls refuse to hear me out. Madame Delphine and Joanna believe that I didn't know anything about Charlotte, and I think the betas do too, but no one else does.

I've heard the girls talk about their own nightmares. Nobody is going to get over this easily. Our lessons have continued as normal, with Madames Delphine and Vivien filling in for Lucille. Out of everyone, I'm still certain that Madame Vivien hates me the most. A few times a week she singles me out again, and I endure her workouts without complaint. I'm getting stronger and faster, and I keep hoping I'll gain her respect, or at least her forgiveness, but nothing changes. She looks at me as if I'm the lycanthrope, as if I decapitated Lucille myself.

I don't have the heart to tell her that I enjoy the punishing workouts. It's the only thing that clears my head. And besides, they're all probably right to hate me—I should've seen the signs. But then again, Charlotte should've asked for help, and the wolves should've checked for bites the first time. Ryne was right when he said he's to blame too. There are many of these "shoulds" floating around the manor these days, but none of them can bring the dead back to life.

It's Saturday morning, so we're permitted to sleep in, but I can't handle being in this room for another second. I need another grueling workout to empty my mind. I peel myself away from the bed and peer out the window. The waxing moon is still in the sky, getting bigger every day, but the sun is rising. That's all I need. I quietly slip into my workout gear and head out for a run. On my way, I stop in the entry to catch up on the scoreboard.

Now that four more girls are gone, I've dropped back down into the bottom of the group. I'm not surprised, not after the past seven weeks I've had struggling with letters, failing at music, and even leaving my canvas blank during most of the art lessons. I haven't given my all anymore when we've had combat training on Thursdays. I've tried to bring up my very valid points again in front of the other girls, hoping they'll back me up, but the men continue to tell us to be patient and *trust the process*—which has to be the most infuriating phrase on the planet. All around, I'm disappointed. My name being in the bottom placement is expected, but it still stings.

What am I thinking? I shake my head to snap myself out of this downward spiral.

I'm being selfish. There are only sixteen of us now. It's hard to believe we've already lost six girls, but we have—seven if we count Willow, which I do. I should be grateful to be alive, not wallowing over my low score. I need to get my determination back. I need to find my grit again before I end up in a mating house.

"I know you were trying harder," Madame Delphine says, and I jump. "But you seem to have lost your spirit again."

I spin to find her watching me from the top of the stairs. She's already dressed for the day in the ugly maroon gowns the house mothers wear. She comes down and stands right next to me. She looks older and softer than I remember with more creases around her eyes and more gray hairs. I see her daily, but that doesn't mean I really look at her. I've been in my own world so much lately that I hardly notice anyone anymore. And right now, there's something in this woman's eyes that appears to be sympathy. I try not to read too much into it.

"Looks like I'm at the bottom again." I frown at the scoreboard.

"I know." She pauses. "What happened with Charlotte has been hard on you."

"Yeah, and I only have about a month to move up." I squeeze my hands into fists. "I don't want to go to the mating house."

"You are a strong woman. I don't think that will be your fate."

I snort, wishing she'll prove to be right. "Even if I manage to climb farther up the board, none of the betas are going to choose me at the next harvest. I'm not pretty enough."

"Honey, if it were just looks the betas were after, we'd place you all the first night."

"Well, I'm not talented either. All these lessons—singing, dancing, music, art, reading. I am terrible at everything. And I just don't get why it's so important."

"It's the custom," her voice trails off and then lowers. "But it's also a way for them to keep the pack strong. The hierarchy among the human women mirrors much of the hierarchy among the wolves. The mating houses aren't created equally, and it's no secret that the beta wives get to enjoy luxuries that aren't afforded to the others."

I think about that for a minute, tying together what she's saying with what she's not saying. If they make us earn our spots in the upper class, make us fight tooth and nail to get a husband, then maybe we'll help them keep this system going instead of trying to dismantle it. Things are starting to make sense now, and my stomach hardens.

Madame Delphine clears her throat and steps back, donning her professionalism once again. "The betas also want women they can relate to and enjoy spending time with, women who are strong against our enemies and who will be loyal to their husbands, no matter what. Who wouldn't want to hold an intelligent conversation with their spouse? You're very smart, Poppy, more so than you give yourself credit for."

"Thanks," I whisper. I didn't know how much I needed the compliment until it was mine.

"These are all areas that you shine in. I believe Anders already has his eye on you, and I'm certain once you start spending time with the others, your score will go up."

I swallow hard. I don't want Anders and can still feel his grimy hands on me. The one good thing about the last few weeks since the full moon is that we haven't seen the betas as often, and the dates were postponed. Nobody will tell us why, but I believe it has something to do with the war going on between the wolves and the lycans—something happened that night, and our men have been extra busy ever since.

"We're starting the dates today." Madame Delphine pats me on the shoulder. "And the betas get to add points for your behavior. I'm certain you'll do well."

The front door opens, breaking the otherwise still morning, and Madame Delphine and I spin around. Ryne sticks his head in, followed by a very pretty woman. Appearing perhaps in her late twenties, she has wide blue eyes and long blonde hair that falls in soft curls around her face. I wonder if she's the wife of a beta. She certainly looks the part.

"Mother," Ryne says, kissing her on the cheek. The woman gives a slight curtsy. "I've brought you Lucille's replacement. I think you will find her very capable."

Madame eyes her warily. "Oh my, you're young. When did you retire?"

The woman clears her throat. "Yesterday."

I expected her voice to be breathy or soft, but she speaks with command and authority. She'll have no trouble gaining our respect, but she still seems too young to be staff here compared to the other house mothers.

"Welcome to our home. Meet Poppy, one of our girls."

"Hello, Poppy." The woman smiles and then flicks her eye up to the board as if she's done it before, which I'm sure she has. She scans it until her eyes land on my name, then holds out her hand. "I'm Nova. Perhaps I can help you escape my fate. We will see what we can do about getting you to rise up on the scoreboard."

I nod, liking her already. "Thank you. I can use all the help I can get."

Ryne won't look at me. He hasn't said a word to me since our argument, and that feels like eons ago now. He stands near me though, and his musky smell lingers in the air—hinting of snowstorms. We only get a few snow-falls each year, but the smell is so unique, so clean and crisp. It covers the rest of the world. That mixed with cedarwood is Ryne's scent, and I have to fight the urge to close my eyes and breathe it in. So instead, I study his black hair and the way it's tied back at the nape of his neck, accentuating his high cheekbones. His jaw clicks, and his shoulders stiffen. He knows I'm watching him.

Madame Delphine clears her throat, and I snap my eyes back to the ladies, my cheeks instantly going hot.

"It's nice meeting you, Madame Nova." I turn and

head out for my run. I can't stand being near Ryne and not talking to him, let alone finding myself wrapped up in his presence when he can't even be bothered to look in my direction. I slip out the door, the scent of snowfall all around me despite the amber sunrise.

Joanna fluffs up her hair. It's getting longer and is close to hitting the top of her shoulders. It still looks great, but I can tell she's bothered by the odd length.

"How do you think she managed to leave the mating house so young?" she asks.

I shrug. "I don't know." Everyone has been talking about Madame Nova all day. We didn't have any lessons with her yet, but she observed all of them. She sat next to me in reading class and helped me sound out words. I still can't read full sentences, but something about her enthusiasm made me think that maybe I'm not a lost cause.

"Why am I even bothering to get ready? I should be helping you," Joanna says.

She retrieves a navy-blue gown from the closet and holds it up against my body. It's got a plunging v-neckline in the front *and* the back. I'm not sure how comfortable I'll be wearing something so revealing, but it should draw attention, and isn't that the point?

We're doing our first group date this evening, and all

the girls are in a frenzy. The betas are taking us out for dinner, and we were told to dress our best. The entire house is a flurry of activity as the girls get ready. Thankfully Joanna and I have this room to ourselves.

"I don't even want to go on this date. What if I get stuck with Anders?"

"Then you get stuck with Anders. It's better than the mating house."

"Joanna! You saw him grope me. You know how he killed my sister?" My voice shakes. "He touched me in the exact same way that he touched her."

"That's brutal." She frowns. "But I still think being with Anders is better than living in a mating house. Anders is the type to go to the mating houses even when he's married. But if you're at the mating house, he'll be able to do whatever he wants with you, but so will a thousand other men."

I glare at her.

"You know I'm right," she huffs. "Don't shoot the messenger. Now sit. I'll do your makeup."

We spend the next hour doing hair and makeup and then head into the foyer with the rest of the girls. The betas haven't arrived yet. There are sixteen of us but only five betas, so the tension grows thick with each new girl to walk into the foyer. Joanna is dressed in black— she purposely didn't choose her best gown, but she looks amazing anyway. She gets Grady all to herself, so the rest of us will be going in groups of four. The top four girls on the scoreboard get to choose their dates. The rest of us will be chosen by the betas.

Madame Nova comes up next to me, now wearing the maroon dress the house mothers wear. It looks odd, aging her at least ten years. "What beta have you had your eye on?"

I let out a breath. "Anyone but Anders."

She raises an eyebrow. "Okay. Good to know."

The door opens, and Ryne walks in first. I didn't realize he would be here, and my breath picks up speed. His eyes land on me, traveling down my neckline and back up again. They lock with mine, and I hold them, daring him to be the first to break eye contact. He does, quickly shifting his gaze to the rest of the women. Anders is just behind him, followed by Nico, Cade, and Justin. They're all dressed in suits and look great, but I can't seem to pay them any attention when Ryne is in this little room, especially not when he is dressed up like that.

The men scan the room, clearly enjoying the array of beautiful young women. Nico stiffens and lunges across the room toward me. I yelp and stumble back just as he grabs Madame Nova, studying her face as if committing it to memory. "Mine," he says and smashes his lips against hers.

Gasps erupt across the room. Anders is there in

seconds, ripping them apart. Madame Nova breaks away breathless. Her eyes shine as she looks up at Nico.

"Nico, she's barren," Anders hisses. His face has gone red, and his entire body is so rigid that I'm certain he's about ready to explode into his wolf form.

"You think I care?" Nico scoffs. "Have you ever heard of a wolf denying his true mate?"

Ryne raises his hands with a little frown, and Anders deflates. Everyone turns to Ryne, waiting for him to say something. All the while, Madame Nova hasn't said a word, but her face has drained of color. "She won't be able to bear you children," Anders says, as if that should outweigh a man's fated mate.

"We don't know that," Nico replies. "Maybe since she's my fated, she'll be able to bear my children. But I don't care either way. I'm taking her." He turns to the alpha. "Will you stop me?"

Ryne shakes his head.

"I thought I was done doing sexual favors for wolves." Madame Nova snaps out of it and pushes back against Nico.

Joanna snorts. "Go, Nova," she whispers.

Madame Nova glowers at Ryne. "You promised I would have this post. I do not wish to be anyone's wife, fated or not. Are you going to break your word to me?"

The tension grows thick as everyone holds their breath. Nobody challenges the alpha, let alone a woman.

It makes me like Nova even more. "I cannot deny any wolf his fated mate," Ryne says at last. "It's pack law."

"And how do you know I'm truly his mate?" she questions. "He could be lying."

"It's not possible to speak a lie about someone being a fated mate to another member of the pack," Ryne says simply. "Our pack bond wouldn't allow it. I assure you that Nico *is* your mate."

Madame Nova turns her glare on Nico. "I cannot bear children, and I do not wish to be with another man for the rest of my days."

"But it's meant to be." Hurt crosses Nico's expression, like she's breaking his heart even though he doesn't know more than her name. The bond of mates must be more powerful than I thought. I can't imagine looking at someone and instantly knowing I'm supposed to be with that person for the rest of my life. But I also can't imagine turning into a wolf. There are a lot of things about shifters that don't make logical sense.

"Please," Nova relents. "It would weaken the Carolina Pack to take me as your mate." Her hand sweeps toward the rest of us girls. "There are many here who want nothing more than to be your mate. Wonderful girls who would be able to bear you a brood of boys and make you happy. Choose one of them and leave me alone."

Nico runs a hand through his mess of chestnut curls and finally lets out a growl. "Fine."

But I don't believe him.

I don't think any of the girls believe him.

Come time for the harvest next fall, Nico won't be selecting any of us as his mate if he can help it. But he's also one of the kinder men here, and he's not going to force himself on anyone against her will.

"Under one condition," he adds, inching closer to Nova. "You come live with me for the rest of this year." If there were any last shreds of hope in the room, they evaporate. These two are practically a done deal, and even though her mouth thins and her eyes narrow, we all know it's only a matter of time until she gives in to fate. That's the way these things go. "I don't expect you to touch me," Nico continues. "You'll have your own room, and you can spend your time as you wish. If you hate the life I have to offer you, then you can leave, and I will choose one of these claimed at the next harvest festival. I'll never bother you again."

She juts her chin. "And what of my post here?"

"I'll bring you here each morning and take you home each night." It's an easy solution. "I'm here often, and besides, a lot of the staff come and go for their shifts. There's no reason why you should have to live here to do your job."

She considers his words. "You promise that if I refuse you at the next harvest, you will never bother me again?"

He reaches his hand toward her to seal the deal. "On my honor as a beta."

They shake hands.

But it's pointless. They're *fated,* and Nico is charming and handsome. Nova may seem determined now, but Nico's got nearly ten months to chip away at her resolve. Look at Grady and Joanna. She insisted she'd never let Grady touch her, but by the next full moon, she kissed him.

The rest of us girls exchange frustrated glances. Our eligible betas just went from four men down to three.

As *my* fate would have it, I end up on the date with Nico. All the girls at the bottom of the list got stuck with the least desirable beta—the one who's gunning for someone else. There's no point to this date. We're fill-ins for the real thing, and Nico can't even be bothered to pretend. Not that I blame him. I don't want to pretend I have a chance with the guy, either. I saw the moment he realized Nova was his fated mate—it was as if he'd woken up for the first time in his life. Nobody will ever compete.

At least the next date will be rotated to one of the other betas. Hopefully, Justin or Cade. I want to avoid Anders for as long as I can, on the chance that he'll fall for one of the other girls and forget all about me.

After the situation with Nico and Nova is decided,

we get our date assignments and are driven to a tall colonial red-brick building overlooking the river. Inside, we discover that our betas each have a floor to himself to entertain his group of girls. We're on the third floor, and though the view of the sparkling river at night is stunning, I'm jealous of the laughing and chattering coming from above and below. Our sad group sits quietly eating, because whenever one of us tries to engage Nico, he mutters a flat yes or doesn't respond.

Pointless.

I twist the noodles on my dinner plate around and around my fork, sighing heavily until I can't take it anymore. "If you'll excuse me." I rise from my chair. "I need to attend the ladies' room." Nico brushes me away like an annoying gnat, and I hurry from the table. I head down the wide curving staircase to the main level and stop short to find Knox bounding toward me. He's alone.

I press myself against the wall.

He stops too, looking around for a minute to make sure we're really alone. "I would hug you right now, but I don't want to die."

To hear his voice directed at me is like a slap across the face.

Tears well in my eyes. "Are you okay? Are they treating you well?"

"Better than most, but that's only because Ryne took a liking to me a few months after I arrived last year." He bites his bottom lip and lets out a deep sigh. "Are you okay?"

I shrug. I'm not okay. I'll never be okay. But Knox has enough burdens to carry and doesn't need me added to his load.

"Listen," he whispers low, voice growing urgent. "I hear things in that car, and there's something you need to know about Ryne."

"What?"

Footsteps pound the stairs below, and he grimaces, shakes his head once, and then continues up the stairs to disappear around the corner. My face burns, and my mind races. I want to chase him down and demand answers. I want to forget this moment ever happened.

I can't have either.

Ryne appears on the stairs. He doesn't smile. "What are you doing, Poppy?"

I swallow hard as my heart skids. I'm afraid to say the wrong thing, but lying to Ryne also feels wrong. "I was just heading down to use the bathroom."

"There's one on each floor."

"Oh, I didn't know that. I only saw the one on the main floor." I turn back around, Ryne joining me as I head back up.

"How's it going with Nico?" He digs his hands into his suit pockets. He's dressed as nicely as the betas, which is strange considering he's not the one dating us. I don't know why I wish he were. It's impossible and stupid. And anyway, I'm supposed to be mad at him for not giving us the proper defense training we need.

"About as well as you'd think dating someone who is fated to another would go," I deadpan.

I don't know why, but I expect him to offer condolences or to at least have something else to say to me, but he doesn't. He veers off at the second floor like I'm nothing of importance and leaves me without another word.

CHAPTER 20

KNOX'S WORDS haunt me the next day—or rather, what he didn't get a chance to say. What would he possibly think I need to know about Ryne? Not to mention those first-love feelings came roaring back during our brief moment alone together. My dreams were filled with memories of our stolen kisses and the way his hands felt on my body, of the dances we shared and the good times we spent with our families.

It's confusing, especially considering what Ryne does to me, but I don't want to think about Ryne right now or ever. Seeing Knox didn't have a big effect on me until he talked to me, until he *looked* at me, and now everything feels different.

I don't want a beta. I want Knox and the life that was stolen from us.

And I can't have either.

The girls congregate in the entryway staring up at the scoreboard. Our points from the dates must've been added in. Joanna and I hit the bottom of the stairs and find our names. The betas could give us anywhere between zero and ten points.

Of course, Grady gave Joanna ten. She's still at the top. Faye squeals because it looks like Justin gave her ten points as well. All the girls who had dates with Nico got zero points, so we're all still at the bottom, and everyone else is lightyears ahead of us. How is it fair that Nico even got to rate us at all? He doesn't care about us.

Joanna frowns at me. "We gotta do something about this. You can't go to a mating house at the next festival."

"I'm trying."

She pulls me to the side and whispers, "I know, but maybe we need to sabotage the other girls."

I step back and gape at her. She's serious. I don't like that idea at all. She isn't talking about sabotaging Faye or the girls at the top, which happen to be the meanest of the bunch. It would be Callista or Ivy. They are the closest to the bottom and my date companions with Nico. Ivy is a distillery girl and is close with Faye, so she hasn't been too kind, but it's not like I want to go out of my way to hurt her. As much as I don't want to be sent to the mating house, I don't want to be responsible for sending someone else either.

"I can't do that," I respond. She opens her mouth to argue, but I shake my head. "I couldn't live with myself."

She tuts. "Why do you have to be such a good person?" We laugh and head outside for our workout.

I was hoping we were running today, but yoga mats are spread out across the lawn. I hate yoga. It's the one physical activity that I'm not good at. I don't have the patience for it, nor am I very flexible. The doors open behind us, and the betas all walk out, wearing workout clothes. They don't normally exercise with us. Double groan.

Madame Delphine stands in the middle of them. "Your dates will still be on Saturday evenings in groups until after the wolf moon, but during the week, the betas will be pulling each of you out for one-on-one time. They will integrate with your lessons. Today they've decided to join us for physical fitness. Tomorrow will be art. We have worked out a schedule, so you will each get individual time with at least one beta every week."

Nico is near the back, talking with Nova and ignoring the rest of us. She's stiff and standing at a distance, but I can already tell she's warming toward him. Her cheeks are pink, and her eyes look brighter than when she arrived here yesterday. I hope I don't get stuck with him again and end up with more low scores.

Justin skips down the stairs and stands next to Faye. They grin at each other, and I'm pretty sure she must have kissed him to get her ten. It's not lost on me that someone as awful as her would already have a beta after her. I wonder if we can count him out now as well. This keeps getting harder and harder.

That leaves Anders and Cade. I search Cade out, finding him hanging back from the others. He hasn't taken an interest in anyone yet, from what I can tell. He's not so bad. He's attractive enough, muscled and tall, with dark skin and black curly hair. He has a stunning smile when he actually uses it. I try to catch his eye, but he doesn't notice me.

I take a step down the stairs, ready to head to the mats closest to him, and a hand grabs my arm. I jerk my eyes up.

Anders stares down at me with a hungry look in his eyes. "You're with me today."

I bite my tongue because I can't afford to lose any more points. At least there isn't much talking we can do in yoga. It's a pretty solitary sport.

I give him a curt nod and head to a spot in the middle of the field so we'll be surrounded by everyone else.

He chuckles. "Wait. I know you don't like yoga."

"How do you know that?"

"We've been watching all of you since you arrived. I know that you enjoy running and hand-to-hand fighting. You hate reading and are an abysmal artist. And Ryne told me you like horses. It just so happens that I have horses at my home." He straightens. "Most of the betas live in town, but I have my own estate farther out. I hope to show it to you someday."

I blink at him. I don't ever want to see his estate, and I certainly don't like to think about Ryne talking to any of the betas about me, let alone this one. But this is not the Anders that I know. He's acting almost nice. "Why are you telling me this?"

He leans forward, and his brown shaggy curls fall into his eyes. He's older than the rest of the men, but not so old that I wouldn't find him attractive. If things had been different, if *he* was different, then I could see myself going for him. "Come on, Poppy, you know I like you." When he smiles, a dimple appears in his left cheek.

A sense of foreboding crawls up my spine, and my inner voice screams at me. I want to tell him to leave me alone, but that would probably make him want me more. I bet he's one of those guys who likes a chase. If I start acting sweet toward him, maybe he'll tire of me, and I can score some good points in the meantime.

He places his hand on my lower back, and I worry that his hand will travel farther down, but he's a perfect gentleman as he guides me away from the yoga mats. "Why don't we run today?"

I step away from him and force a smile. Running doesn't require any touching. "That sounds nice." Excitement shifts in his icy eyes, and I immediately wish I hadn't agreed.

A hand slips through my elbow, and Joanna stands there with Grady. "Are you guys jogging? We'll come with you."

I release a sigh of relief.

"This is supposed to be one-on-one time," Anders growls.

"Relax, man, we're all just talking," Grady says with a grin. He winks at me, and I wonder what Joanna has told him about my hatred of Anders.

I'm tired of all the chit-chat. I extract myself from Joanna's grip and take off in a jog, figuring whoever wants to come with me will.

Anders quickly catches up and runs next to me. Joanna comes to my other side with Grady next to her. No one says anything. That's fine by me. I don't have to talk while I'm running.

"I heard that the girl who changed into a lycan was your roommate," Anders says.

My jaw tightens. "Yes, and I should've seen the signs but didn't."

Grady snorts. "There are no signs. I doubt even Charlotte knew except for the bite. She would've had zero symptoms until the night of the full moon."

"That's not what everyone thinks. They're all mad at me, even Madame Vivien."

"That's not right," Anders says. "We'll talk to her. Maybe we should do a class on the lycans and explain how they can hide in plain sight."

He smiles, and that damned dimple appears in his left cheek again. His sweetness is throwing me off guard. I'd much rather he be his true self around me than put on his act.

"Yeah," Grady agrees. "I want Joanna to be able to fight them."

"I already can, you moron. I wasn't helpless at home, you know."

"I know. But extra training can't hurt. You have to be able to protect our pups."

She growls. "I'm not having your babies."

Grady rolls his eyes, and I almost do the same. Joanna likes him—she's admitted as much to me. "You were singing a different tune on our picnic. Didn't you tell me that our first child would be named Daniel after your father?"

"No. I told you *my* first child would be named Daniel. You are such an imbecile. I don't know why I even kissed you."

Grady chuckles. "Because you looove me."

She punches him in the arm, which only makes him laugh even harder as they fall behind. They keep their eyes on me but give us space.

Anders has grown quiet.

"Do you wonder if you'll ever find your fated mate?" I ask.

He scoffs. "I doubt it. It's rare. The fact that there have been two this year is a miracle. And I'd rather not be fated. I'm not ready to settle for just one mate for the rest of my life."

At least he's honest.

"Isn't that the point of betas choosing a mate?" I already know the answer is no, but I want to hear it from the source.

He snorts. "The point is to keep the pack hierarchy stable, but after our women retire from childbearing, I'm free to choose a different one."

I have to force myself not to roll my eyes. "Have you had a mate already?"

"Yes. Three actually. My last one retired a couple of years ago. I have eight children. Nico is my son."

I stop abruptly and gape at him, trying to wrap my head around that. This news leaves me shocked, and I thought nothing could shock me anymore. He doesn't look much older than Nico.

"I know what you're thinking, Poppy. But shifters age slower than humans. Our average lifespan is close to two hundred years." He shrugs like it's nothing.

"So how old are you?"

He puffs out his chest and edges closer to me. "I'm ninety." Old enough to be my grandfather! And he only looks about a third of that age by human standards. It makes me wonder how old Ryne is, but I don't ask. Faye said Ryne's twenty-three, and I'm inclined to believe that, but what if he's older? What if he's already had a mate who is now retired too? My mind swims with questions, and I'm suddenly filled with suspicion that the wolves have been lying to us about everything. I don't know who to trust anymore or what to believe.

"How do you feel about Nico being fated to Nova?" I ask, my voice cracking.

That angry streak of his flashes across his face, and then something else. Love? No. Not that, but some kind of twisted version of love. "Nico wasn't born a beta. That honor went to my eldest who's already with his second mate. Nico is my youngest, so he's always been special to me. He joined the lower ranks when he turned fifteen and had to claw his way to the beta rank, which took nearly a decade of hard work. He was driven by wanting to bring up sons of his own and make me proud. And now he's drooling over a barren woman like some kind of virgin pup. It's despicable. He should contribute to the pack and carry on our family legacy, but I can't do anything about a fated mate."

I swallow hard and step back. Anders scares me. I hate him for killing Willow and I'm afraid for anyone who has to be near him. He can go from violence to charming within a matter of seconds. I'm suddenly very aware that Grady and Joanna aren't paying us any attention. They're farther back on the path, kissing against a tree, wrapped up in their own world.

"Ryne told me that you frequent the mating houses." I blurt out the first thing that comes to mind, instantly regretting it. I don't need Anders thinking about a mating house while he's practically alone with me.

"I do. Just because we betas have a mate doesn't mean we have to give up the other pleasures of life."

Bile rises in my throat. This man is disgusting. He could have had Willow either way. He could have chosen her for his mate, or if no one else did, he could've had her at the mating house. But she fought his roaming hands, and he killed her for it. And now, what does he think? That I'm going to be with him? That I'm going to forgive him for ruining my life? For destroying my family? And if I am with him, that I'll just stand by so he can sleep with other women—women who are being forced into sexual slavery?

I turn away and begin jogging again. I can't stand to look at his face a moment longer. He catches up and runs alongside me as if he has no idea what I'm thinking, or maybe he does, and he simply doesn't care.

Or maybe he likes it.

"I'm sorry about your sister," he says at last.

My heart twists in surprise. "No, you're not."

"That's not true." He grabs my hand and tugs me to a stop again, giving me an earnest expression. His icy eyes shine. Regret is not something I've ever seen on his face, and I hate him even more for it now because I know it's nothing but a practiced manipulation. "I lost my temper. Emotions were high with the harvest moon and the claiming. They got the better of me. Once we shift into our wolf form, we become more animal than man. I regret my actions."

"What am I supposed to say here?" My cheeks burn.

"Do you think there's a chance you could ever forgive me?"

No. That will never happen. I can't forgive murder, especially one so brutal, especially my twin sister. But I don't say that because even though it's true, two can play this game. I have to think of my future. Perhaps he'll help my score if I'm nice to him. "Maybe."

"I'll take a maybe." He smiles again and pulls me into a tight hug. He smells of sweat and wet dog and everything I hate.

I hug him back and force myself to sink into him. It takes every ounce of self-control that I have not to rip away.

He needs to think he's winning, that I'm one more woman he can control. He can't—this isn't over. I will never forgive him for murdering Willow. He's a bad person who cheats on his wives and replaces them when they can no longer bear children. He kills the women who resist him; I'm sure Willow isn't the first and won't be the last. When the moment is right, when he's least expecting it, I vow to return the favor.

CHAPTER 21

THE FULL MOON comes and goes without incident, and the following month is a blur of dates and lessons. Luckily we're still doing group dates, so I don't have to be alone with Anders. My scores aren't improving enough to keep me out of the bottom. Every morning I check the board, only to be disappointed. I'm trying to stay positive—I'm working hard—but the fact remains that I'm not cut out to be a beta wife.

"Today we're going to have an important lesson on pack hierarchy," Madame Delphine says one morning during breakfast. "Finish up. There are outfits laid out on your beds. Please go change and meet back in the foyer."

We're only a week away from the Wolf Moon Festival, and my name remains on the bottom. The madames constantly remind us during lessons that the bottom two girls will be sent off to the mating house the night of the festival. It's meant to motivate us, but I'm starting to panic.

"You can still get your score up. There's still time," Joanna whispers to me as we rise from our seats. I nod once and glance over to Faye and Ivy. Ivy's also at the bottom. They exchange a conspiratory look and then turn on me, both of them smirking. I'm not willing to sabotage other girls, but I can't say the same for everyone else.

"Don't worry about them," Joanna says. "I won't let them hurt you."

I sigh, wishing she could guarantee that.

Many of our lessons are in the classroom, and I expect this one to be the same, but the outfit I find on the bed is a long red cotton sweater dress with a sophisticated white hooded wool coat to layer on top. Thick black tights and little black booties complete the look. It's all brand new, as if it were made specially for today.

"Okay, we can definitely make this work," Joanna gushes, picking the dress up and pressing it to her chest in a little hug. For as much as she hates this place, she adores the clothing. I guess that makes sense given her background.

We hurry to change and go to the foyer where Madame Delphine leads the lot of us outside. The sky is dreary and overcast, which explains the identical warm outfits. We near the river to find the same boat from our first day waiting for us. The engine rumbles gently in the water, sending ripples into the wake. We climb inside and sit on the rows of wooden benches. It's not as crowded since there are four fewer of us than there was the night of the harvest moon. One more week, and two more will be off to the mating houses. Unlike last time, there is no sense of excitement today. Not even the distillery girls are into it. The only thing I can read on their faces is dread. Somehow we all know today isn't going to be a good one. Maybe the dresses were meant to placate us, or maybe they were meant to make us easily identifiable.

"Where are the betas?" Ivy asks.

"We'll see them there," Madame Delphine says. "Madame Vivien will be staying back at the house." Madame Nova is the last to climb into the boat, and even she looks worried. "So it's just me and Madame Nova here today. Please don't stray from our group once we get to the city."

I force a smile on my face and sit up taller, catching Madame Delphine's eye. Others may not be happy about this day, but I've got a score to increase. If faking a positive attitude and sucking up to the house mothers is how I'm going to do it, then so be it.

We're off, and it gets even colder. I huddle close to Joanna as we bounce across the water. It feels like forever until we finally dock in the historic part of town. It's beautiful here, the history well preserved and untouched from the years of neglect like other parts of the city. I can almost picture what it must have been like before the wars. I can imagine the human families who lived here, free from fears of lycans or shifters. This is nothing like the tall shiny buildings with the mating houses and where the pups are raised. It's nothing like the outskirts of the city where things are falling apart, or like the villages where life is simple. It's similar to the area where we gathered for the harvest but nicer. I didn't know homes like this existed anymore.

We're instructed to walk down the sidewalk in a single file line, to keep our heads high, and to smile. As we pass several of the homes, women and their male children peek out. Some of the people wave at us, and we wave back.

"These are the betas' residences," Madame Delphine announces. "Some of you will live in this neighborhood."

"It's amazing," Faye gushes. "Can you tell us which houses belong to *our* betas?"

"We'll leave that for another day," Madame Delphine replies with a sly smile. "Come along, now."

Madame Nova heads up the rear of the group, and Joanna and I slow down to chat with her. "So you're living with Nico in one of these?" I ask. "What's that like?"

Her mouth thins. "It's nowhere I belong. I'll be staying in Drayton Hall full time soon enough."

"Right . . ." Joanna's voice dips into sarcasm. "You do know that he's been marking all his dates with zero points, don't you? He has no intention of marrying one of these claimed girls."

"Our agreement isn't about what he wants. It's my choice." Nova brushes a bit of lint from her dress. "Don't worry about Nico. And anyway, you have Grady."

"Yeah, and Poppy here has nobody."

I elbow Joanna in the ribcage. "It's not her fault."

Madame Nova frowns. "I'll see what I can do. I'll talk to Nico about what he's been doing with the scores."

"It won't help Poppy. She already went on her date with him, remember?"

Our group stops in front of a white home. It's by far the nicest one in the neighborhood, with plastered walls and tile roofing. I've never seen a home with these kinds of materials, and I instantly fall in love with it. "It's called Spanish style," Nova says, as if sensing my thoughts. "There's a few like this around here, but this one is by far the biggest."

I peer up at the three stories of arched windows and terraces, columns by the front door, and the towering palm trees in the yard, and something twists inside of me. It's immaculate, and I long to know what it looks like on the inside, but I know that even if I do, it won't matter.

"Which beta lives here?" One of the girls asks the question we're all thinking.

"This is the alpha's home," Madame Delphine supplies. "It belonged to Ryne's father, but since King Tremaine runs the Chicago Pack now, Ryne lives here alone."

So that would mean Madame Delphine used to live here too. She only had one child as far as I know. I wonder what it was like for her to be with someone who left her when her child grew up. She went from living in this beautiful home as a lady to running Drayton Hall for the claimed young women. There's definitely a story there.

"But we're not going inside Ryne's residence today," she continues, pointing across the street. "This way, please."

We cross the little cobbled street to an open area with grass and trees—a park. We have one at home in the village, but it's nothing as grand as this. There's even a playground that's laid out like a castle—ours was a single slide and swing set. Little boys play on it, some in wolf form, others as humans. We keep walking to the far end until we come upon a crowd of men and a few women who are so dressed up that they must be beta wives. The crowd is loud, and a nervous energy seems to crackle through them. Something important is happening.

We walk toward the crowd, but before we reach it, Madame Delphine stops, gathering us around her.

"Who can tell me the hierarchy of the wolf pack?"

My hand shoots into the air. The madames occasionally question us, awarding points to the girls who answer correctly.

Madame Delphine nods to me.

"The alpha king lives in Chicago, ruling over all the shifter cities. Each city has its own alpha; Ryne is ours." I pause for a moment. When I lived in the village, I would've never thought of the pack as part of my life. I would have called him their alpha, not ours. And now, it's practically all I think about. "Below him are the members in the Council of Betas, who are all mated. They advise Ryne and oversee the unmated warrior betas."

"And who are below the betas?" She raises an eyebrow.

This is where it starts to get tricky, but I'm pretty sure I have it. "Next are the gammas. They are the defensive warriors who protect the wolf city and the surrounding human villages. And then below them are the deltas. They have the greatest numbers. They can be hunters, but they're mostly the offensive warriors who leave to fight the battles out in the wilds."

"Very good. How many are in each class?"

My hand shoots up again, but so does Faye's. Madame Delphine calls on her instead. "The council usually has between twenty and forty betas. That depends on how many are currently mated. The unmated warrior betas are always one hundred. When a beta moves up to the council or dies, a gamma takes his place."

"And do any of you know how many gammas and deltas there are?"

This time, Ivy's hand is the first one up. "There are exactly three hundred gammas, but the alpha can assign more if he feels the pack needs extra protection. The rest are deltas, and I think there's got to be at least a thousand of those by now."

I swallow hard, trying to relax. I had no idea there were so many wolves. They act like they're so outnumbered by the lycans, but I can't imagine that's actually true. And to think, the girls in the mating houses have to sleep with any man who wants her, an endless parade of partners who care for nothing but sex and growing the pack. They don't even know who their own children are most of the time.

It's not right.

I raise my hand, and Madame Delphine points to me. "So, if most of the children are raised by the pack, how do they choose which ones become deltas or gammas?"

Her lips thin. "That's a good question. There are levels to the mating houses, which helps keep things organized from birth, but there are also opportunities for the boys to compete for the gamma spots during their fifteenth year."

"And what about the girls?" I can't help but ask.

"You said one in a hundred wolf shifters is born female."

She nods. "If she's born of beta parents, she'll be permitted to stay with her family. If she's not, she'll be sent to Chicago to be raised in a special boarding house overseen by the king."

I look around, noting the surprised faces of some of the other claimed. Either they weren't paying attention, or nobody told them the truth. Maybe I shouldn't have asked my questions—it'll only create more competition—but we all deserve to know what will happen to the children we'll one day have.

The shyest girl of the bunch raises her hand. Her name is Bailey, and she mostly gets by because she doesn't have any enemies, and she keeps her nose in a book most days. "So I know the children are raised by the pack, but when do the mothers get to visit them?"

Nova bristles. "Never," she grumbles. "And you'll be right back to mating after you recover from childbirth."

The mood visually shifts, some girls staring at their shoes and others with mouths hanging open like fish.

Someone needs to stand up to the alphas. Not just to Ryne, but to his father. I want it to be me, but to think things will ever change is laughable. There are far too many wolves, and what are humans supposed to do about it? My family doesn't even know what's happening in this city. They think I'm some kind of servant. If they knew what service I was training to provide, they'd be horrified.

"Enough about that." Madame Delphine clears her throat and continues. "Two more questions before we join the crowd. How does one become a warrior beta?"

Lexi, the teacher's pet type, beats me to it. Which stinks because she's not far above me in the rankings, and those points could've moved me up one slot, but then again, I'm starting to feel sick to my stomach and don't care to talk anymore. I want this lesson to end.

"Any wolf wishing to vie for a spot above them in the pack hierarchy has to fight for it," Lexi says. "In this case, several may fight for the spot of beta, but only the last one alive gets it."

I frown. The wolves are so desperate to grow their packs that they'll harvest human women, but then turn around and fight each other to the death? It seems like such a waste.

"That is correct to a certain degree. A wolf may surrender during a fight, but if they do that, they will be cast out to live as a lone wolf in the wilds. It's the greatest shame that can happen to a wolf, and most would rather die." She levels us all with a steely look, but I can't understand why. "It's the same process for those deltas wishing to move into the spot of a gamma. Gammas typically live longer lives because they get to stay closer to home. They also get better accommodations and are permitted more visits to high-quality mating houses."

The fact that they put us into different levels of mating houses is disgusting, as if women need to be ranked. It reminds me of the farm animals that get entered into competitions at some of the villages that surround ours. Every spring Papa would take us to see the winners. Bile burns in my throat, and I have to relax my face to keep the anger from showing. There are over a thousand wolves just in the delta class, and I wonder how many mating houses there are. The one Ryne took me to was large, to be sure, but there couldn't have been more than twenty or thirty girls there.

"We will be visiting the battle arena later this evening where the deltas, gammas, and warrior betas fight each other. Now, last question. How does a beta become an alpha?"

I answer before she can even call on me. "They challenge the alpha to a fight. If they win, they take over the pack, but if they don't, they die. There is no option to surrender."

"And how do they win?"

"They kill the alpha."

"You girls have been paying attention. And now you are about to witness a challenge on our alpha."

"How often does this happen?" Faye asks.

"It's rare now. Maybe once a year. Sometimes not even that. Ryne is a strong alpha. You are lucky you get to see him fight."

We follow her toward the crowd, and all I can think is that I certainly don't feel lucky.

CHAPTER 22

THE CROWD of wolves parts for us as we approach the circle. They all nod to Madame Delphine, but a few sneer at us girls. Madame explained that challenges against the alpha are always in the park near Ryne's house because he gets to set the time and place, and he likes to go home afterward and rest. I also wonder if it's a way to intimidate his challengers, as if he can't even be bothered to battle in the arena. This is his home turf.

We shuffle forward until we are right in front. Ryne stands shirtless at the far end of the circle, and he gives his mother a tight smile. The wolves in the crowd are restless. Joanna squeaks next me, and I look over to see that Grady has come up behind her and wrapped his arms around her waist, pulling her back into his broad chest.

"Are these all beta wolves?" I ask him.

"Yes. Only warrior betas today. Except the two standing behind Ryne. They are council betas sent to witness."

"Who challenged him?" Joanna asks.

"That idiot Braden. He became a warrior beta less than a month ago. He doesn't stand a chance. But he's not the risk to Ryne. It's those who will challenge him afterward."

"What do you mean? Madame Delphine made it sound like it'll only be one."

"That's how it starts but fighting weakens him and wolves can be opportunistic. Ryne will probably fight four to five betas tonight as more come forward to try for a shot at alpha. I don't know why anyone would risk it. Ryne is a monster. He's unbeatable. The real fun comes later. We'll go down to the arena and witness the brawl that will bring in the new warriors."

"That sounds barbaric," I say.

"It is. But it's part of our world. Yours now as well." He squeezes Joanna tighter. She shakes her head but doesn't say anything. I sure hope she doesn't think this is *fun*.

Ryne steps forward, and a hush falls over the crowd. A young guy stomps from the onlookers, his fist pumping in the air as if to get them to cheer him on. Nobody does, but it doesn't deter him. He smiles wickedly and flexes large muscles as he rips off his shirt. This must be Braden.

"Do you challenge me?" Ryne asks him with an annoyed glare.

"I do," Braden replies haughtily. He puffs out his chest before crouching into a fighter's stance.

Both men release guttural screams and shift into their wolf forms, their pants ripping to shreds in the process. Ryne's wolf is unmistakable—I'd recognize that perfect inky black fur and those glowing sapphire eyes anywhere. He's actually smaller than Braden's wolf. Braden is raggedy with tufts of brown fur mixed in with the gray, but he's massive and rippling with excitement. They growl and circle each other for only a moment.

Ryne makes the first move.

He pounces, landing on Braden's back and sinking his teeth into the hide around Braden's neck. Braden wails and tries to buck him off, but Ryne holds fast.

The crowd is cheering now, egging Ryne on. Braden falls to his forearms and then flips over, putting himself on top of Ryne. It works long enough to get Ryne to release his hold, and then the two are back up and circling each other again.

Blood drips into the grass. Braden is hurt. He growls and lunges for Ryne, this time swiping at his shoulder and getting a hit. Ryne isn't the slightest bit deterred. He attacks again, the anger rolling off his wolf in waves of absolute dominance. It's obvious he's done this many, many times before.

It doesn't take long.

Ryne gets his mouth around Braden's neck again and shakes violently. Something in the gray wolf cracks and dislodges, and Braden tumbles to the ground. His body is completely limp. He never even had time to shift back to his true self, not even in death. Or maybe this wolf is his true form, and the human form is the lie.

Ryne howls and then shifts back. He's naked. His muscled back is to me, and blood drips from the wound on his shoulder. He calls out again. "Do you challenge me?"

Another man tears from the crowd, shifting instantly into a scrappy gray wolf. Ryne shifts again, and the fight is on.

"I guess a council beta decided to end his life today." Grady sighs. A middle-aged woman screams obscenities the entire time, begging her husband to stop, but before long, it's Ryne she's begging to stop. Of course, neither do until the gray wolf joins Braden in death.

The woman falls to her knees, her dress billowing around her. Her sobs will probably be heard for miles as she's carried away. Once again, Ryne shifts back into his human form and calls out for more challengers to come forward.

"Nobody would dare," Joanna asks Grady, "would they?"

But before Grady can reply, two more men step forward in answer. They appear to be very young, and they're obviously identical twins. They're both fair-haired and lanky. My heart does a little twist. They remind me of me and Willow.

Ryne's shoulders slump. I can tell he doesn't want to do this. "Who's first?" he snaps. "Or would you like to die together?"

And that's all it takes.

The boys shift into identical honey-colored wolves and circle their alpha. I almost expect him to make them fight one at a time—that's fair—but he doesn't.

He shifts into his wolf form once again and goes for the closest of the two, ripping into the much smaller wolf with unrelenting teeth and claws. He's so fast that, even with two of them, they still don't stand a chance. One jumps on his back, but Ryne is quick to shake him off, slamming the young wolf to the ground. The wolf whimpers and then shifts into his human form.

"I surrender!" the boy calls out.

A dissatisfied murmur ripples through the crowd.

The other wolf uses the opportunity to pounce on Ryne. He lands on the alpha's back, getting a tight hold of Ryne's neck and biting down, same as Ryne has done to the others. Ryne roars and shakes the wolf off, but not without taking a deep gash to his neck first. Blood glistens on his black fur.

Ryne turns on the wolf and delivers the killing blow. He clasps his jaw down on the exact right spot to split open an artery. It ends his opponent in seconds. As his lifeblood spills, the wolf turns back into a boy. He looks barely old enough to be here. Maybe sixteen at most. His twin crawls over to the dead brother, looking up at Ryne with blood on his face.

"Please," he begs. "I shouldn't have listened to my brother. It was his idea. I never wanted to do this. It was stupid. Please, please have mercy."

The crowd goes silent. Ryne is still in his wolf form. He looks up and catches the eye of a man I hadn't noticed until now. The man is standing at the far end of the crowd and is surrounded by massive betas who could be bodyguards. He's dressed in a black suit, but even without that, power would still radiate off of him. He's clearly someone of importance.

He also looks just like Ryne, if Ryne were a little older.

"That's the alpha king," Grady whispers, confirming what I was thinking. "Name is Thorn Tremaine."

"I knew it," Joanna whispers back.

"My sons are fools." A middle-aged man steps to the edge of the circle. "I beg you to spare my child, but I know that you probably will not." He kneels down. "Still, I must try. Please."

Ryne stands there, still in his wolf form, leaning over the crying boy. The alpha king nods once to his son. That's all it takes. Ryne acts, swiping a claw along the boy's neck. It slices clean through the flesh and ends him quickly. There isn't even time for the boy to scream.

CHAPTER 23

THE ALPHA KING smiles and melts into the crowd of betas.

The man who was moments ago begging for his son's life crawls forward and holds his dead children in his lap, crying silently. Never once does he blame Ryne. There is no anger in his eyes, only deep regret.

"Disgusting," Joanna whispers.

"This is the way of things," Grady replies, his voice clipped. "We're wolves." As if that's justification.

Ryne stands firm in the middle of the crowd and howls. It's starting to get dark. The sun is setting fast. We all wait to see if another wolf will step forward in challenge as minutes pass. No one does.

Ryne changes back into his human form. Sweat streams down his chest, and blood is everywhere. I drop my eyes and immediately regret it because now all I see are the four dead souls strewn about the grass. Anders hands Ryne a towel, and he wraps it around his midsection.

"Go enjoy the brawl. I'll see you all tomorrow," he calls out to the onlookers.

He stalks toward us, and the crowd parts, letting him through. As he walks past me, making eye contact for a half a second, I have an overwhelming desire to go to him. I step forward, but Joanna grabs my wrist and jerks me back.

"What are you doing?"

I don't answer her because I can't explain it. I hate him, but I can also see the pain in his eyes and can't help but want to comfort him.

Once he's past the crowd, the spell breaks, and a sickly kind of excitement fills the air. Grady drops a kiss on Joanna's cheek. "I've got some business to take care of. I'll see you at the brawl. Save me a seat."

She sniffs. "Fat chance." But I know she will.

Madame Delphine waves us over. "We'll ride over to the brawl with the rest of the betas. Feel free to mingle among them. They will behave. I promise." She winks. "It's time you started to get to know more than just the four who might be your mates. We will meet back at the boat after the brawl."

Joanna pulls me back. "Now is our chance," she whispers so low I almost miss it. "By the time she realizes we are missing, we'll be long gone."

"What are you talking about?" I ask.

"You are at the bottom of the scoreboard. In a week you'll be on your way to a mating house. We can't let that happen."

"But you're at the top. Plus, you're so in love with Grady. You can't leave him."

"I am not in love with him. It's an act. I don't want to be here. Never have."

My mouth drops open. She had me fooled, and I can't help but wonder if she's lying to herself. I see the way she looks at Grady.

"I won't let you go to the mating house, and you'll never get away on your own. Now come on," she hisses.

I need to be stronger, braver, smarter—this is my chance. A few weeks ago, I'd never have taken it, but now a strength is rising inside of me, one that started as a flicker and is building to an inferno. Joanna is right. It's time to run.

I don't think as we melt into the crowd, our group of girls getting farther and farther away. I have no idea where we are going or how we'll get there, but at least it won't be a mating house. My fear of the wilds is nothing compared to my fear of living in one of those places.

We slip away from the crowd under the cover of darkness and into the shadows of two quiet houses. I loved this outfit when I first put it on, but now I hate it. It makes us stand out. I can only hope that it's dark enough, and the wolves are preoccupied enough, that our red dresses and white coats won't become a dead giveaway.

"Let's stay here until the boat leaves," Joanna says. We listen to them laugh and carry on as they all get on the boat. There's more than just our group as many betas have joined in. The boat is packed. It rumbles to life and begins to move down the river, disappearing into the night.

"Do you think anyone saw us?" I ask.

She shakes her head. "They would've come after us if they did." The lights in the houses next to us are both off. I didn't think when we decided to escape, but now panic is setting in. If they catch us, they'll kill us.

"Maybe we should go find help and pretend we got separated from our group," I say. Nerves are eating away at my belly. That and we're wildly unprepared. We haven't eaten for a while, we have no food or water to take with us, and we're in these stupid dresses. This is a terrible idea.

Joanna grabs my arm. "No. We'll be fine. Trust me."

"Do you even know where we can go?"

She doesn't say anything.

"You don't have a plan?" I'm having a hard time keeping my voice down, and I'm already regretting my moment of courage that led me here.

"Of course I have a plan," Joanna hisses low. "I just can't tell you everything in case we get caught. I know where we are going, but I'm not telling you."

Her words sting and it bothers me that she doesn't trust me, but then again, I lost my nerve and argued for going back. Joanna grabs my hand and tugs me out of our hiding spot. I feel exposed, but there is no one around.

"What if someone sees us?"

"Then we pretend we're wives of betas."

"And if the people we run into know all the wives?"

"Stop worrying. We'll get out of here. I promise." Her voice is growing frustrated and impatient. She tugs me down the street, approaching Ryne's house. Every light is on, and I shrink into the shadows as we pass. Joanna sniggers a bit. "You know, if I didn't know better, I'd think you were sweet on him."

"What? No." And besides, I think the alpha king is in there. That man scares me.

She loops her arm through mine and tugs me closer to her as we walk down the street. If anyone saw us, they would just think we were two friends out for an evening stroll. I'm glad Joanna has a good head on her shoulders because if it were me, I would just flat-out run, which would look suspicious.

We make it a couple more blocks, and the knot in my chest releases. We're getting closer to freedom. Has Madame Delphine realized we're gone yet? Probably not. There were so many people piled onto that boat, and she said we would all meet back *after* the brawl. She's not keeping track. We have hours until the brawl is over. At least I hope we do.

A lone man walks on the sidewalk, heading straight for us. I tense.

"Relax," Joanna says. "We'll be fine. Just don't make eye contact."

I drop my eyes and giggle like Joanna has said something funny. The man slows as we approach, coming to a stop. Joanna keeps our pace, which is good, because I would've frozen. He doesn't say anything, and as soon as we pass him, I hear his footsteps start up again. I let out a breath as he disappears.

"That was close," I say.

"Nah. Not even. He didn't even notice us."

"Then why did he stop?"

"Because he assumed we were beta wives and was being respectful." Her voice drops an octave. "We will have to cross the river. That's going to be the hardest part."

"Do you mean like swim?" I gulp. I'm a good swimmer, but it's freezing cold in January, and the current is strong. Visions of drowning wash through my mind.

"What do you think I am?" she scoffs. "There are people who will help us. Trust me."

I don't know why I never thought someone would help us, but I truly didn't. The idea that there are people out there who feel the same way we do, people who would risk their lives to get us out of this city, gives me hope like I haven't had in months. A smile plays on my lips, and adrenaline pumps through my veins, encouraging me onward.

We pass several dark houses, and out of nowhere, a hooded man steps out from between two of them. Joanna and I both stop, and then Joanna gives a nervous laugh. "Goodness gracious, man, you scared us."

My heart thunders in my eardrums, and I ready myself to run.

She moves to step around him, and he lashes his hand out, gripping my arm. "Where are you going?" he growls.

I know that voice. "Ryne?"

Joanna pales. Ryne uses his other hand to peel away his hood, and his ice-blue eyes glare at me. My breath catches, and I try to wrench away, but his grip is impossibly tight.

He drags me back down the street, and Joanna jogs to keep up. I want to tell her to run, to get away while she can because Ryne obviously doesn't care what she does. He's singled me out. I don't know what will happen to us now. Hopefully Ryne won't kill us, but I don't really know. Is this it? Is this the end? Maybe he'll throw me in the mating house and be done with it. I've certainly caused him enough trouble, and it would be easier to get it over with. But as he marches me down the sidewalk, I think it's more likely he'll kill me.

"Are you taking me to the mating house?" I bite out.

He snorts but doesn't say anything.

"Please, Ryne, you don't understand," I press on. "We can't live like—"

"Shut up," he finally hisses. "Don't say another word."

It takes no time at all for us to reach his house. He pulls me up the porch steps and shoves open the front door. Joanna stumbles in after us. Knox stands in the entryway, his eyes wide. His face drains of color, and I wish for so many things in that moment—for him to help me, for him to get away from me, for him not to have seen me like this at all.

"Is my father gone?" Ryne snarls.

Knox nods. "He's left for the brawl."

"Good. Go fetch Grady, but don't tell him why I need him. No one knows these two are here but you and me."

Knox disappears out the door. I'm overcome with betrayal. I know it's stupid, and Knox can't do anything for me now, but his loyalty to Ryne stings.

Ryne tosses me down onto a couch that is way more comfortable than any I've ever sat on before. Joanna sinks down next to me. There's a long pause that seems to go on forever. My breath slows, and my mind starts to relax. Maybe he's not going to hurt us. I close my eyes tight and count backward from ten, then open them and allow myself to look around. His house is stunning. The style dates back to well before the wars. It's gorgeous with dark wood and papered walls. Beautiful paintings adorn the walls. I run my fingers along the edge of the white couch pillow—the furniture is upholstered with a mix of white linens and creamy leathers. I suck in a breath and catch his smell, that winter and cedar scent. It does something to me I don't like, so I close my eyes again. I'll never be in a room this nice again in my life. He's going to send me away to a mating house. I can feel it. And if for some reason he spares me, I'll end up there in a week anyway.

Joanna elbows me in the ribs, and I open my eyes to see Ryne pacing in front of us. His hair is wet and hangs around his face, hiding much of his expression. He pinches the bridge of his nose. There are still scratches all over him, and blood is seeping through his shirt.

"Explain," he finally says.

My mouth goes dry.

"We were leaving. I couldn't stand around and let Poppy get sent to the mating house," Joanna says matter-of-factly. I'm surprised she didn't try to lie to him, but Joanna is a straight shooter when she wants to be.

"So you decided to run away?" He curses under his breath.

"It's not like we had any other options. Poppy has been at the bottom of the board for weeks, and the festival is coming up."

"You would've died out there."

"We were willing to take our chances. Better dead than forever raped by wolves."

Ryne doesn't speak; he just continues pacing. "I get it," he says at last. "I don't like it, but I get it. Joanna, do you have any idea how devastated Grady would be if you left? You can't mess with him like that."

He claims to get it, but then he cares more for his friend's feelings than our own. I fold my hands over my chest and glare. "What's our punishment? Because if you are going to kill us, please just get it over with."

"Now she speaks." He snorts. "I'm not going to kill you, but if you ever try this again, I will bring your family to the city and kill them in front of you." He stalks over to me and leans down close. "Do you understand?"

My stubbornness is shattered to pieces with his words. I cower away from him and let out a clipped yes.

"Good. You're damn lucky nobody else knows about this because that's exactly what would have happened if you'd been caught by someone else." He stands back up. "Don't you get it? I wouldn't have had a choice."

I think of Mama and Papa and little Evan, and my stomach goes hollow. "You would punish them because of me?" I'm choked up. I can't help it. It's so wrong.

He shakes his head angrily. "There are things about being an alpha that I can't control, and I'm not going to be able to keep protecting you if you keep making reckless choices like this."

Protecting me? He's done nothing to protect me.

"Now, the reason you ran away was because you don't want to get sent to the mating house, yes?"

I nod meekly.

"Okay. Then I will tell Madame Delphine that Grady wanted to spend some time one-on-one with Joanna and that I requested you join her. I will instruct Madame Delphine to give you just enough points so that you are third from the bottom after tonight. You have a week to not screw that up. Do you think you can handle that?"

I have no idea why he's decided to be nice to me. I feel like there is a catch here somewhere, but I can't find it.

Joanna scowls at him. "Why are you being so nice to her?"

Leave it to Joanna to say what we're all thinking.

"Because I want Grady to have a shot with his fated mate, and that seems to only be possible if Poppy's around."

Something inside of me deflates. Again, he's only "protecting" me because it's important to his beta. Ryne looks out for his friends, and normally I'd find that admirable but not in this case.

Joanna crosses her arms and smirks. "Damn right it is. You hurt her, and I will raise hell."

I mean, it's a nice sentiment and all, but I can't help but feel that's not the reason Ryne is helping us. There's got to be something else going on, but for the life of me, I can't figure out what it is.

Knox comes back into the room with Grady in tow.

"Joanna?" Grady asks, shaking his head. His sandy hair catches the light, and his silver eyes darken with worry. "What's going on?"

"They tried to run away."

Grady's face pales, and in that moment, I swear I can see his heart break.

"You what?" he says, still staring right at Joanna. Then he brings his gaze back to Ryne and swallows. "Would you like me to get their families?"

Ryne shakes his head. "We're going to keep this between us for now."

Grady visibly relaxes. "And what are we going to do about it?"

"I'm not going to do anything. Whatever you wish to do with Joanna is up to you. We have an hour or so before we have to head to the brawl."

Grady grips Joanna's arm, pulling her up from the couch.

"Hey, let go of me. I'm not your property."

"You have no right to speak to me in that tone right now," he yells. "What were you thinking? You could've been killed! I should kill you myself!"

Joanna cowers. It's the first time I've seen her scared of any of them. Grady drags her out of the room. I want to chase after them, to defend my friend, but somehow I know Grady isn't going to harm his fated mate. Of all the betas, he's the kindest, and he's obviously in love with Joanna.

"What will he do with her?" I ask, just to be sure.

He shrugs. "He won't hurt her, though her pride may be bruised a bit by the time he's done. My guess is they'll be making out the next time we see them."

Knox leaves and comes back into the room carrying a steaming bowl of water. He holds my gaze, his eyes full of intensity. The energy in the room shifts, and Ryne jerks his head around. "Leave it. Poppy will clean me up."

CHAPTER 24

KNOX GIVES a wordless nod and sets the bowl down on the little table next to where I'm sitting. He pulls a couple of washcloths and bandages out of his pockets and lays them next to it. And then he's gone. I have to admit I'm disappointed, but I understand; Knox is trying to survive the same as any other human, and I doubt Ryne wants him around while I handle this. Guilt washes through me when I realize I don't want Knox around for it either. I'm pretty sure Ryne doesn't really need my help. I mean, he's been through this how many times now? Regardless, I gaze at the first-aid supplies, deciding where to start. I've doctored up my little brother plenty of times and even Papa once when he cut himself in the field.

But I have no idea what kind of care Ryne expects.

He unzips and shakes his arms out of his jacket and

then peels off his bloody t-shirt, muscles rippling in the process. He's clean from the shower, but there's a lot of blood seeping from his wounds. Aside from a nasty gash on his neck, everything looks minor.

He sits down next to me. I don't move.

Ryne looks at me for a long moment before clearing his throat. The side of his lips curves up playfully. "Poppy, will you please clean my wounds? I'm not good at it myself, and I just sent away my man."

"Oh, yes."

Heat prickles over my skin. I dip one of the rags in the water and set to work on the worst areas. I clean up the big gash on his neck, only to find a wound right cutting across his stomach as well. My fingers graze over the hard ridges as I work. There is something strangely intimate about this, which leaves me feeling unnerved, and yet I can't help my attraction to him. Why does he have to be so alluring? Why do I have to both hate him and want him at the same time?

He hisses as I wash the stomach wound, but he doesn't complain. I rub some ointment over it, then place a band-aid on top and set to work on his arms. The cuts are much smaller here and don't need much. Never once does the man move. It's like touching a warm statue.

"You know what Joanna said about the mating houses?" His voice is low and soft. "About being raped by wolves? I wish it wasn't that way."

"You would do away with the mating houses?"

He shakes his head. "We have to have them in order to procreate, but I wouldn't force women there. We would recruit from the villages but allow women to volunteer and be paid. I actually expect we'd have more women than we do now if we did it that way. I told my father that once, but he thought I was joking."

He's wrong. I can't imagine anyone volunteering for that. Well, Faye maybe. But his words surprise me.

"I didn't realize your father had so much control over you."

He sighs. "You have no idea. I am an alpha to others, but my father is the alpha to me, which often means I'm just as trapped as you are. I have no control over who my mate will be either. He'll choose her."

"Why?"

"Because he wants a strong mate for me. I understand it, but I don't like it."

I move back in front of him, washing away the rest of the blood from his chest. He locks eyes with me, taking my hand in his and peeling the washcloth from my grasp, then pulls me closer to him. My lungs tighten. Traitorous excitement spreads through me like hot liquid.

In spite of all logic screaming at me to run away, I don't. I allow him to pull me down into his lap. He stares deep into my eyes with his stormy blue ones before leaning forward and placing a soft kiss on my cheek. I let my eyes flutter closed and revel in the moment. Tonight I'm not a claimed woman waiting for a man I'll never love. Tonight I'm just a girl enjoying the touch of a man I'll never have but desperately want.

I marvel at how quickly he can take my emotions from one end of the spectrum to the other. He moves his face up and gently kisses both of my eyes. My heart leaps. He feathers his lips down the other side of my face and runs his nose along my neck. I bring my hands up and twist my fingers through his hair.

He lets out a little moan and pulls me closer to him.

Bringing his lips to my ear, he whispers, "I know you don't think this, but you are the most beautiful girl I've ever laid eyes on. From the moment I saw you, I wanted you. But I can't have you."

"Why not?" I squeak, and my cheeks warm.

"There are plans for me that don't include you, but I swear on my life that one of these days, I will kiss you."

I gasp, longing to pull his lips to mine.

He sighs. "But that can't be tonight. I don't want to make you a target."

I swallow and try to make sense of his declaration. Up until now, I've been denying my feelings for him, but I can't anymore. I know who he is, and I want him anyway.

"Okay," I breathe out. I don't want to agree. I want to demand he kiss me and put us both out of our misery, but I'm not brave enough.

He pulls away and sets me to the side, lifting me off his lap as if I weigh nothing. I instantly miss his touch.

"Poppy, I promise I'll do whatever it takes to keep you out of the mating houses. I don't know how yet, but I will. That means you'll end up with one of my betas, but that's better than the alternative."

I swallow. "Thank you." But I don't mean it. Anything short of being with him will be wrong.

He lies back on the couch, and a wicked smile crosses his face. Before I can blink, he pulls me on top of him again. He holds me and plays with my hair. Our bodies are pressed close, and neither of us says another word. At first I'm filled with electric need, but contentment starts to creep in, and I relax. We lie there for who knows how long until I drift in and out of consciousness.

Someone clears his throat, and I bolt up. Grady stands there, smirking, and Joanna's eyes are wide. I notice a distance between them that has never been there before. They must still be mad at each other.

"We have to go," Grady says. "Or Madame Delphine will send out a search party for them."

Ryne runs a hand over his face. "Knox, bring me a shirt," he calls out. I force myself off of him, not wanting Knox to see me so close to his captor. Ryne takes the washcloth again and cleans up the last of the blood. His wounds have completely healed. I knew the shifters healed quickly, but to see it myself is shocking.

Knox enters the room holding three different shirts. I

can't meet his eyes. Shame sweeps over me, and I've never felt so confused. Ryne grabs a black t-shirt, slipping it over his head.

"Come on, let's go."

I stand and follow them out the door.

"Where to, boss?" Knox asks. I wince at Knox's cheerful tone because I know it's fake.

"We have to take these women to the brawl. It looks like they're going to have to meet my father after all."

We ride across town in the back of Ryne's car. Grady is still seething mad, so he chose to sit up front in the passenger seat. He doesn't look back or speak a word to Joanna. She's folded in on herself and staring out the window, equally angry. I don't know what happened between them tonight, but whatever it was only made things worse. I'm squashed between Ryne and Joanna, and every inch of my left side burns with the memory of the time we just shared. It's an odd feeling, wanting to lean into him with Knox only a couple feet away. He drives us through the city, and when I catch his gaze in the rearview mirror, he quickly averts his eyes.

Is he mad at me for trying to run away? Is he upset that I got caught? Or can he sense my draw to the alpha?

I'd give anything to have a moment alone with Knox, just to talk. I'm afraid that will never happen. The incident on the stairs was bittersweet. Sweet because we were finally alone together, and bitter because it ended so fast.

Ryne shifts his weight, and his arm presses against mine. I can't help but study his smooth tanned skin. It's a marvel, really . . .

"What?" he asks.

"Your cuts and bruises. They're gone so fast."

He nods. "Benefits of being a shifter. The only thing we can't heal from is a lycan bite."

"Not the only thing," Joanna murmurs.

"That's right, Jo," Grady speaks up. "We're not immortal. We bleed. And we die. Just like what would have happened to you tonight if Ryne hadn't saved you."

"Saved me?" she growls. "That's a funny way to put it."

"Enough," Ryne interjects. "You will behave. We're here."

Sure enough, we slow to a stop outside of a large structure unlike anything I've seen before. It's tall and concrete, curving around the edge, with bright lights at the top. I'm not sure what it is. Knox jumps out to open the doors for us, and we climb out. I gaze up at the building, feeling small.

"It's a football stadium. Used to be used for human sports," Knox says.

Ryne shoots him a scathing look, and Knox backs away, holding his hands up. "I'm sorry, Alpha. I forgot my place."

Ryne doesn't say anything. He takes my hand and

tugs me after him. "Is Knox not allowed to speak to me?" I ask.

He stops short and tilts his head, giving me a suspicious look. "How do you know his name?"

White-hot fear shoots through my body. "You've used his name many times in front of me."

He frowns. "Right. Sorry."

I don't want to get Knox into trouble. They'll kill him if they think he's trying to start something with me. I'm certain of it. Everything they do here is about growing the pack. A claimed man cannot have a claimed woman. They're here for labor, and that's all. There aren't many of them since only the human families who never had daughters have to give up a son, but I hate that any of them are here in the first place. As far as I'm concerned, the deltas could be doing these jobs, and the human men could be spared from a lifetime of slavery.

And a lonely existence.

Knox gets back in the car, and his face disappears behind the dark glass.

Joanna and Grady walk on either side of us as we head toward the stadium entrance. They won't even look at each other. I'm sure it won't last. Joanna can hold a grudge until the end of time if she wants, but Grady is smitten. He'll forgive her and work his way back into her heart. At least, I hope that's what happens for both of their sakes.

As we go inside, the first thing that hits me is the

noise. The men holler and cheer so loudly it's like walking into a wall of sound. The next thing is the smell, crisp winter night mixed with sweat and blood and alcohol. And the third is the blinding light. I blink rapidly until my eyes adjust. I wish they hadn't because what I see is horrific.

CHAPTER 25

THE BUILDING IS open to the dark sky and shaped like an oval. Most of the seats are empty, but there are still globs of people cheering from the raised seats all along the sides. In the middle is an open field of grass with bodies strewn across it.

Too many bodies to count.

Wolves and naked men lie sprawled out, many with their entrails exposed. Tears burn my eyes, and I drop them to stare at my shoes.

"Looks like it's over," Ryne says with a twinge of something in his voice that's either regret or relief. Regret that he missed it or regret that it even happened? I wish I knew.

"Are you sure you don't want to go down there?" Grady asks.

"Yes. Let my father announce the new rank advancements. He loves it."

"He'll be sending the ones who surrendered out to the wilds," Grady says, spinning to Joanna. He grabs her chin, turning her to look at a line of four men on their knees on the far side of the field. "Do you know what would have happened to you if those rejected wolves had come across you out there?"

Her face turns stony, and she jerks away.

"Come on," Ryne says, "let's go sit down with the other claimed."

We make our way down several sets of stairs until we come across Madame Delphine and the others sitting in rows near the edge of the field. Our girls are intermixed with the betas, some who are courting us and some who are not. All the girls have smiles on their faces, but even I can tell that most of their smiles are fake. I wonder what atrocities they witnessed tonight. I'm suddenly grateful for Joanna's impulsive heart, even if it meant we got caught. At least we didn't have to watch all these men die.

We join the others, and Faye shoots me a disgusted look before sitting on Anders's lap. A few rows above, I catch Justin's longing gaze on her. I somehow know that her attention toward Anders is all part of her master plan. If she can make Justin jealous, then he'll want her even more. Nova and Nico are sitting side by side, their heads bent toward each other in a deep conversation. Nova can say she's not going to marry him, but there's no getting between those two already, and it's only been about a month. Cade is in the middle of a group of six girls, all vying for his attention. From the satisfied smirk on his handsome face, he's obviously loving every moment.

I glance at Ryne, wishing we could be public with our affection here. I want it to be like it was back in his house when we were alone, but one look at his pained expression, and I know that's a foolish thought. I'm not supposed to want him. He's bad for me. Even he's starting to come around to that fact.

The four of us sit down with the others as Ryne's father struts onto the field. He announces the new positions to a wave of cheers from the audience. When I don't immediately react as the others do, Ryne elbows me in the side. "Play along," he whispers against my ear. "It's for the best, trust me. If my father doesn't like you, you're as good as dead."

I clap and smile and fake it along with everyone else because when the alpha king wants you to clap, you clap.

When the time comes for the four surrendered wolves to be exiled to the wilds, things take a dark turn. "I've never had respect for cowardice." The king's smooth baritone voice rings out over a speaker, echoing through the stadium. He sweeps his hand around to all the bodies. "At least these men died heroes. You four are a disgrace to this pack." He stalks toward the four cowards so angrily that I think he's about to shift into his wolf and end them himself. "I've decided it's only fair that you battle each other for the right to live. The last one standing will be allowed to go to the wilds. The rest will die along with your more courageous brothers."

The men look at each other with shock, but it doesn't take long for the battle to begin. They dive for each other, their forms turning from man to wolf in midair. The crowd loves it.

"This is new," Grady says low over the roar of cheers.

Ryne is stiff as a board beside me.

"Carolina is your pack," Grady continues to him. "Are you really going to let him change the rules like this?"

Ryne's wolf growls from within, and he turns on Grady. "Not another word, beta."

Grady shrinks back. "Apologies, alpha."

Joanna looks between the two and rolls her eyes, a little bit of her personality thawing underneath the icy attitude. For the first time, I realize that Ryne may be afraid of his father, and I want to know why. I peer over to Madame Delphine, but her face is an unreadable mask as she watches the field. The poor woman has to watch the man who was once her lover and her husband and the father of her child, and act as if he is nothing to her now. I don't blame her for hiding her emotions. She gave him an heir and an alpha, and what was she given in return? A new job grooming the upcoming claimed. Madame may well be a respected title, but she's not living the life of an alpha's wife, and certainly not the life of an alpha king's wife.

The entire time the four men battle, I keep my eyes downcast. I can't watch. I only know it's over by the way the crowd cheers louder and the people around me stand and jump and scream. I stay planted in my seat, and Ryne stays with me.

"It's over, Poppy. You'll be able to go home now," Ryne whispers. The word home hits me like a punch in the gut. "I'm sorry about this. I wish it could be different."

"Why can't it?" We're surrounded by standing, cheering people, who are paying us no attention, and somehow it feels like we're the only ones here. I stare at him, taking in the tangle of long raven hair around his tan face, the high cut of his cheekbones, and the deep blue of his eyes. It's a face I could stare at forever, and right now, I think he understands. More than that, I think he might agree with me. He cups my cheek and wipes away a tear that I didn't realize was trailing down my skin.

"It just can't." He peers into my eyes, pleading for me to understand. But how can I ever understand? He claims he's just as trapped as I am, that he doesn't have control, but I don't really believe that's true. He has a whole pack of shifters who will do whatever he asks.

"Hello, son," a gravelly voice interrupts us. "I didn't expect you to come out tonight." Ryne drops his hand from my face and turns as the voice continues. "Are you going to introduce me to this woman who seems to have stolen your attention?"

The crowd parts to reveal the alpha king standing not three feet away from us.

CHAPTER 26

RYNE MOVES AWAY from me as we stand. I'm not sure why he doesn't want to be seen with me in public, but I'm certain that whatever the reason is, it'll hurt me. If it didn't, then there would be no reason to keep secrets. I frown at that, wishing I were better at guarding my heart from him.

Joanna is at my side, looping her arm through mine. "Tonight," she whispers in my ear, "you are going to tell me exactly what is going on between you and Ryne."

I nod, too distracted by the power dynamic between father and son to pay attention to what she's saying. They're standing toe to toe, neither one saying a word.

We're all watching.

Waiting.

The alpha king is still dressed in the same pressed

black suit from earlier, though he's loosened the tie, and the sleeves are a little rumpled. Like most of the wolves, he has shoulder-length hair. It frames high cheekbones, same as his son's. There's one streak of gray in the front, but otherwise it's also black as ink. He has the same cerulean eyes as Ryne but with a few added wrinkles around the creases. The resemblance between Ryne and King Thorn is uncanny—nobody could argue Ryne's parentage. Thorn is quite attractive for a middle-aged man, but then again, his middle age isn't the same as ours.

How old is he, really?

Anders doesn't look much older than Nico, and Anders is Nico's father. Not only that, but Nico is Anders' youngest son. So that must mean the alpha king had Ryne when he was much older than when Anders started having children. Maybe King Thorn went through several wives before he found one who could give him an heir, or maybe Ryne has brothers that I just don't know about. Thorn is definitely the oldest shifter I've seen, so maybe that's how he rose to his position. In fact, I don't think I've seen *any* wolves yet who actually look older than forty. Odd, because if they live to be twice as old as humans, wouldn't they at least look elderly by the end of their lives? Maybe the shifter genes don't work that way, or maybe most of the wolves don't make it to old age because they kill each other so haphazardly for rank. Was Thorn Tremaine a shifter during the wars? Did he help fight the final battles that ended the human governments? Did he help establish the claiming of humans?

I'm filled with questions I'm far too afraid to ask.

"I see you've brought along this year's claimed." The king speaks, breaking the tension and glancing around at the girls. When his eyes travel across me, my cheeks prickle. "How many will marry a beta?"

"Five."

"Good thing it's not more. I have to say, son, your houses are lacking a little. You have too many men and too few women. It's time for you to either lower the claimed age or take two from each family like we've done in Chicago."

I force myself to hide my horror. If they took two, that would be twice as many women fighting for the betas. It would not be pretty.

"Perhaps. But I still think you're going to run into human population problems, father. I don't think that's the solution."

"Then what is?" His father chuckles, but he's clearly not amused.

"Maybe it's just time for me to expand my territory. The Savannah panther pack is weak." Ryne sounds so sure of himself. "We could take them out and gain all their humans."

I blink rapidly. Panther pack? I thought only wolf shifters lived in this area. I've heard whisperings of other species of shifters out there, but to realize an entire pack lives close is a revelation.

The king raises his eyebrows. "You would take another city? But, son, that is the stuff of kings, not princes. Are you saying you want to usurp me?" His tone is joking, but his eyes are razor-sharp on Ryne.

"Not at all, I only wish to grow your territory as well as mine. You mentioned that we don't have enough women. If I expanded down to Savannah, I would have twice as many villages to claim from."

The king claps him on the back. "Don't apologize for ambition. I'm glad to see a little initiative from you. Now, tell me. Who's heading to the mating houses on the wolf moon?"

Faye slides forward and loops her arm through Ryne's. Her cheeks are rosy, and her smile is triumphant. She's certainly getting around tonight—the girl thrives on attention "That would be Poppy and Callista."

My jaw drops. I want to punch her square in the nose and rip out all that pretty auburn hair. Joanna squeezes my arm, and I'm sure she wants to do the same.

The alpha king narrows his eyes at Faye, biting his bottom lip suggestively. "And you are?"

"Faye Donovan, Your Majesty. Top of the board. At the harvest moon, I will be a proud wife of one of the betas." She bats her eyelashes. "Unless there's an alpha who needs a mate?"

He chuckles. "I like you . . . So where are Poppy and Callista?"

His eyes roam the crowd, and Callista inches toward the king, her hands shaking. I move as well, but Joanna holds me back. "I have to," I hiss.

I step forward, and Ryne shifts a little so he's standing between me and his father. The alpha king's eyes flash with mirth, but he doesn't say anything. He simply strides around Ryne and places a finger under my chin, forcing me to look in his eyes. No, these are not like Ryne's eyes after all. They are cold and unforgiving and laced with evil thoughts.

"What's one week?" He puts an arm around my waist and tugs me into him. "Poppy will come home with me tonight, and I'll drop her off at the mating house before I leave town."

Ryne bristles. "That's not how things work in my pack, father. Callista and Poppy have one more week to prove themselves, and I owe it to my men to let them have the first taste of the women if they fail." The two men face off a moment before Ryne adds, "Besides, Poppy moved up the board today. Give her a week to see if she can hold her spot."

Callista clicks her tongue, and some of the other girls send me scathing looks.

I know Ryne's trying to protect me, but his words still make me shiver. And now everyone knows he's willing to stand up to his father when it comes to me. I don't know if that's a good thing or a bad one, but I'm leaning toward bad.

The alpha king stares at me for the longest time, and I'm certain he's going to refuse Ryne's wishes. My heart speeds, but I stand tall. "I suppose so," he says at last. He leans down and whispers low in my ear. "I see the way my son looks at you. Next week, when you inevitably enter the mating house, I'll come back for you. I will have you before he does. That's a promise."

He straightens and slips away into the crowd of gawkers. It takes every ounce of self-control I have to not collapse into Joanna's arms. I am now under the alpha king's nose, and I don't see how I can possibly get out of it.

"Delphine," Thorn hollers.

She rushes to his side, curtsying low. "Yes, Your Majesty." It's the first time I've ever seen her completely submissive. She always stands up to all the wolves, but right now she's not even looking this man in the eyes.

"I would love to escort you and your girls back to the manor. Then you and I have things we need to discuss."

He holds out his arm, and she slips her hand through. I wonder if I'm the only one who sees the slight tremble. Joanna grabs my hand, jerking me back to her.

Grady stays with us as we make our way up the stadium stairs.

Faye has not left Ryne's side, and she giggles at something he says as they walk ahead of us. He looks just as easy with her as he had been with me, and my chest burns with jealousy. Perhaps whatever happened between us was nothing.

But it didn't feel like nothing. It felt real. Even more real than what Knox and I had.

And he did just stand up to his father for me. That has to count for something.

"Are you okay?" Grady asks. I jerk my head toward him, surprised. I would have expected the words to come from Joanna, not him. He's barely said anything to me as long as I've known him.

"I'm fine. Why wouldn't I be?" I'm careful to keep my face blank, wishing I could believe my lies.

Grady doesn't say anything more. We walk from the arena through a few city blocks until we're at the river's edge again. We climb into the boat and find seats, and Ryne joins his father. The rest of the betas say their goodbyes. I have a feeling Ryne hadn't been planning on going with us, but he doesn't want to leave us alone with the king. To think that he's the only person in this entire city who can stand up to Thorn is terrifying.

We're all tired by now, the long day bearing down on everyone. Exhaustion clouds my mind, and my eyes want to shut it all away. Joanna sits next to me at the back of the boat, wrapping an arm around me. I wrap one around her too. We don't speak. The boat starts to move—I'm used to it by now—and soon we're traveling up the river. It's dark enough to see the stars since the moon is barely beginning hanging over the horizon. The breeze and mist from the water are icy cold, but I don't mind them because they wake me up.

I watch Ryne—I can't help myself.

He's sitting between his father and Faye. The girl practically has herself in his lap, and his arm is around her back, but he doesn't seem to be paying her any attention. His eyes keep tracking back to me. Even though he's cast in shadows and sitting all the way across the boat, I can still make out his features under the half-moon. I know he's watching, and I like it.

He's beautiful. On the outside, of course, but there's light hidden within his inner-darkness, trying to get out. I want to find it, to show him that it's okay to be good.

Maybe he really does want me. Maybe he really will protect me.

I remember what he said earlier about kissing me one day, and my heartbeat picks up. I can picture us now, can feel the softness of his lips and the hardness of his muscles as he wraps me in an embrace. Everything else seems to melt away, and longing rises up inside of me unlike anything I've ever felt before.

He must sense it because he narrows his gaze, and even from here, I can see the same thing mirrored back in him. Our future kiss is inevitable. We are inevitable. We must be. We have to be. I can't help but smile. For the first time since coming here, I actually feel like I matter and that maybe I'm special.

That's when Ryne breaks our gaze, turns to Faye, and kisses her.

CHAPTER 27

I'M FROZEN, unwilling to believe what I'm seeing, but unable to look away. He's really kissing her, and for everyone to see.

For me to see.

Joanna's arm stiffens around my side, and she curses under her breath. "Don't look, Poppy. He's not worth it."

I rip my eyes away, and my heart shatters. It shouldn't. This is stupid. He's not mine. He's the alpha, and there was no way he was going to keep me around anyway. He would've just used me and spit me back out. He even said that he'd help me get with a beta, and never once did he say I would end up with him. At least I hadn't kissed him. It would've made this worse.

Maybe not though, because then I'd have the memory.

The moment we shared at his house was more intimate than a kiss, though. At least I thought so. I drop my eyes to the boat floor, and my mind swirls. I can feel my face burning as a few of the other girls look back at me.

Ryne keeps kissing Faye.

Joanna puts her other arm around me and holds me close. I have no idea what's happening to me, but tears threaten. I will them away, not wanting Ryne or anyone to see me cry. The betrayal is too much.

Finally, I brave a glance back up. Ryne releases Faye, and she positions herself under his arm, smirking. He doesn't look at me once as he turns to his father, starting up a relaxed conversation. It's like I don't even exist.

Resolve swells in my chest. I've let myself become distracted. If I want to stay out of the mating house, I've got to be focused on the betas. Justin or Cade are the only ones I can even hope to win, and if they were here right now, I'd channel all this emotion into them. I'd get up right now and go flirt with them. I'd let them know that I was interested. My choices are slim, but either of those men would be a million times better than a life in the mating house.

Faye meets my gaze and blows me a little air kiss. She's gloating.

There's something about her that draws men in like a magnet, and whatever it is, I need to find it inside myself. I need to step up and prove to everyone that I'm capable of being a beta wife. Cade would be easier to ensnare, seeing as he isn't already set on Faye, and I'm pretty sure Faye is still planning on Justin. Although, if I were able to snatch Justin from under Faye's nose, that would be justice well served. First, though, I have to work my way up the board.

I hope Ryne keeps his word and gives me enough points to at least be out of the bottom two, but I can't count on anything from him ever again.

Why did he kiss her? The question pops into my mind, and I shove it aside.

The boat docks at our house, and I refuse to jump out of my seat and race off the boat in front of everyone. I walk slowly to the house, my shoulders back and head high, and don't stop until I'm in my room. I strip off my clothes and climb into bed. I don't think I'll be able to sleep, but I have to pretend so I don't have to talk to Joanna when she comes in.

I close my eyes tight, and all I can see is Ryne's lips on Faye's. Despite my best efforts, tears wet my pillowcase that night.

I stop at the scoreboard on the way to breakfast the next morning. Sure enough, Ivy has bumped down a spot, making me third from the bottom. Only two points separate me from her, and ten points are between me and Katelyn for the fourth from the bottom spot. As awful as it is, I'm not too worried about Callista. She doesn't have strong alliances in the house, and none of the betas have shown her any interest. She's just as helpful in the classes as I am, but she's not good at exercise or fighting either. The poor girl doesn't stand a chance.

I can focus on overtaking Katelyn later. For now, I just need to stay above Ivy and Callista. My heart twinges a little because I know what that means for them. I wonder if they truly realize exactly what's in store if I succeed. I'm certain none of the other girls have paid a visit to the mating house because if they knew the truth of it—if they saw what I saw—they'd be fighting tooth and nail to stay out.

Joanna loops her arm through mine in that familiar way of ours, and we enter the dining room. We're the last ones in, and I jerk my eyes over to Faye. I expect her to be crowing about the kiss with Ryne, but she's not. Her eyes are red rimmed, and there's a cut on her cheek and a yellow bruise under her eye. I can't tell from here, but it looks a little like a bite mark. She's got her eyes on her grits and isn't saying a word to anyone.

"What happened to Faye?" I whisper.

"Oh, I forgot you went to bed before everyone. The alpha king wanted to take her home. Ryne refused, so the king took her on a walk instead. The stupid girl went willingly, of course. I was still in the library chatting with Bailey when Faye came running up the stairs. She looked a mess and was crying. I have no idea what happened, but whatever it was, it wasn't good."

I don't want to feel sympathy for Faye, but I do. I can

only guess at what the king did to her. That man is cruel down to his center.

"If he took away her virtue, does that disqualify her from marrying a beta?"

"I don't think anyone would dare question it since she was with the king."

What did Madame Delphine have to endure in her years with him? Maybe she's happy to be running Drayton Hall. Maybe this was her out from a lifetime at his beck and call. I look around for her, but she's not here. It's just us girls this morning.

Normally, Faye has her sidekicks surrounding her but not today. It makes me feel doubly bad for her. Just because someone is popular doesn't mean they have true friends. True friends are there for you no matter what, especially when things get uncomfortable. Right now, all of Faye's friends are staring at their plates and pretending she's not here, which would explain why the only seats left are at her table. Joanna and I sit down and start our breakfasts, but I can only pick at mine.

"I'm sorry about whatever happened to you last night," I say to Faye. I can't help it. I don't like her, and she doesn't like me, but I feel terrible for her. No woman deserves violence like that, and my mama raised me better than to look the other way.

Faye scoffs and drops her fork against her plate with a clatter. "Do you mean the part where Ryne kissed me?" She raises an eyebrow, and the cut on her cheek stretches. "Because yeah, I figured you'd be sorry to see that. But guess what, Poppy? I'm not sorry."

My stomach hardens. Okay, maybe I don't feel so bad for her.

"Why do you have to be such a bitch?" Joanna cuts in. "She was trying to be nice."

"By rubbing it in my face?" Faye glares at me. "Don't make comments on things you'll never understand, little girl."

"Don't talk to her that way."

"Oh, and what's she going to do about it? Poppy is weak."

That comment cuts the deepest because I know she's right. I am weak. I have been ever since I got here. But I'm tired of being weak. I want to jump across the table and show her just how strong I am, but I've realized something lately. Being strong doesn't mean being violent or stooping to her level. Being strong means standing up for yourself.

"I'm not going to sit here and take your abuse. I tried showing you kindness. I'm done." I push back my chair and gather my dish to take it to the kitchen. A wave of relief washes over me. Whatever happens to me, it won't be because of Faye. She has no more power to make me feel bad. The fact is we're in this terrible situation together. She's a victim too. She's really good at making herself seem like the villain here, but she's not. The villains are the Carolina Pack, the alphas, and the whole damn system.

"So that's it?" Faye hisses. She's right on my heels. "You're just going to walk away from me? What about last night?"

I turn on her. "What about last night? Facts are that Ryne kissed you, and then his father hurt you. I don't know what else you want me to say here."

"Do you want to know why he hurt me?" She steps closer. "Because you didn't accompany him to the mating house like he asked." She points to her bruised face. "As far as I'm concerned, this is your fault. It should've been you."

Heat ripples across my skin. "You'd rather I'd be the one with cuts and bruises? That I endured that and who knows what else?"

"Yes."

I shake my head at her. "Why? Honestly, give me a reason why."

"Because I'm going to be a beta wife, maybe even Ryne's alpha wife." She spits at my feet. "And you will be nothing."

CHAPTER 28

THE WEEK PASSES FASTER than I thought it would. Before I know it, the morning of the wolf moon dawns. There are no classes today, but tonight we'll head back into the city for the celebration where the two lowest scoring girls will be sent to the mating houses. Just the thought of it makes me shiver. Dread twists me up inside, but so does relief because at least by tonight, we'll all have some answers.

I throw on a pair of running shorts and lace up my sneakers. This week was good to me—it felt like I could do no wrong. Madame Vivien eased off on her personal training sessions and had us run for physical fitness. In combat class the betas were busy, so we fought each other. I didn't get to throw a punch at Faye, unfortunately, but that's okay because I was the last woman standing. And thanks to Madame Nova and Joanna's tutoring, I'm finally able to read a little bit. The only iffy class was knitting. My scarf turned out completely lopsided, but I still managed to turn out a better one than Ivy's. And both Callista and Ivy are horrible at combat. It doesn't make me feel any better sending women to the mating house who are terrible at defending themselves, but that's not my fault. I can't keep feeling guilty for other people if I'm going to survive this place.

I stop and stare at the board on my way out the door, expecting to see our scores. Instead, there's a note written across it. *Final scores to be revealed tonight. Good luck!*

I take a deep breath and tell myself not to worry. Yesterday morning I was third from the bottom, and I had a perfect day, so there's no reason why I shouldn't be safe. After this, I'm going to work harder than ever to climb up the board and win a beta. The betas have stayed away this week, but Madame Delphine said that was only because they were initiating their new warrior betas and preparing for the wolf moon festivities.

The front door creaks open, and Nova slips in. Dark bags line her eyes, and her lips are pressed tight together. She sees me and forces a smile.

"You're up early on your day off."

"I like to run in the mornings."

"Can I join you? Running is good for thinking."

I glance at her maroon uniform dress, and she chuckles. "I'll change if you'll wait for me."

I nod and slip out the back door, stretching my legs. I like Nova a lot, and she's been generous with the points she's given me, but we haven't really talked much since the day she arrived, besides the extra tutoring sessions. But then those aren't really about talking, they're about learning.

She joins me, and we start slow. I don't know what her pace is, and I don't want to leave her too far behind, but she speeds up a little, and I follow. Neither of us says anything on the first lap, so I startle a little when she speaks up just as we pass the house.

"Nico wants to take me as his mate tonight."

"I thought they only did that on the harvest moon."

"That's what I thought too, but Nico said they can do it at any festival with the alpha's approval. Grady wanted to do the same thing with Joanna, but Ryne told him no. He said Nico and I could make things official, though."

"Do you want that?" I hadn't realized they'd gotten so close. She was so adamant that she wasn't going to be with another wolf again.

A soft smile brightens her face. "I do. But I feel guilty. That's one less beta for you girls. If I agree to be his mate, then I'll be condemning another girl to the mating house. I would never wish any of you to go through what I did." We slow to a walk and catch our breath. "Nico is a good man. He's kind and gentle, and he doesn't care that I'll never be able to give him children. I'm stealing one of the good ones. That's not fair to you guys, and I'm not sure if I'll be able to live with myself."

"But do you love him?"

She wipes a few tears off her face. They've made her blue eyes bright, and when the sun catches her blonde hair, it lights her up like a halo. She looks young and in love.

"I do." She lets out a cathartic laugh. "I've not said it out loud yet. But I really do. I know it's only been a short time since I met him, and it sounds crazy, but this fated mate thing is impossible to explain."

"Try? Because I'm curious."

She shrugs. "I can't not be with him."

"Then I don't see that you'll have any choice. Will you still work here?"

"Yes. We talked about that. Since I probably won't be able to have kids, then it makes sense that I do something with my time. I like working with you girls."

I nudge her. "We like you too."

"But a lot of the girls will resent me."

"Probably, but I won't. And you know what you can do for us?" I sigh deeply. "You can prepare us for the mating houses, not just the betas. Because most of us will end up there, and I don't think these girls have any idea what's in store for them."

Her face pales. "That's true. Maybe I can help. I'll have to be discreet about it, of course."

We jog in silence for a while.

"What beta are you going to try for?" she asks at last, eyeing me with a tilt to her lips.

"I haven't decided yet. I'm not even sure I'll make it past tonight."

She grins. "Actually, don't tell anyone, but you're fourth from the bottom right now. You're going to be fine."

Relief sweeps through me, and I let out a little laugh. "Thank you for telling me."

She nods. "So, back to the betas. Who's caught your eye?"

I think about that for a minute. "Cade is a safer bet, but if I get Justin, I can rub it in Faye's face."

She chuckles. "I've noticed that you two don't get along."

"That is the understatement of the year. I don't know how to win over a man though. Will you help me?" I can use all the help I can get. And, well, she *did* work at a mating house.

"I'm not supposed to show favoritism, but I always love an underdog. Next week, we'll do a makeover, and I'll teach you how to woo a man." She giggles and suddenly sounds as young as she actually is. She can't be more than ten years older than me. Her hard life has aged her, but maybe things are about to change. Maybe they're about to change for me too. "And I'll also see what I can learn about Justin. The more you know about him, the easier your job will be."

Now it's my turn to laugh. "All I know about him is that he's all about having fun and flirting with the pretty ladies."

"Good. Then you'll be perfect."

We're taken to the Wolf Moon Festival by boat an hour before the sun is supposed to set. The pale moon has already risen over the horizon even though the sky is still indigo. As we zoom across the water, the moon looms over us like a promise.

The lycans will be out soon.

I wonder if Charlotte is still out there somewhere and if she made it through the last two months in her new life. I'm sure I'll never see her again, and even though I'm still angry at her for keeping such a big secret, right now, I can understand why she did it.

Because I'm terrified.

Even though I'm in the fourth slot, I still feel like something bad is going to happen tonight to snatch that away from me. Maybe it's this place and this whole messed up process, but I've lost my trust.

"You did it." Joanna squeezes my hand. That girl is good at reading people. I already told her the news, but she can tell I'm still freaking out. "Don't worry. Tonight you can relax and have fun. I hate to say this because it goes against everything I stand for, but I think you should flirt with the betas tonight and really put yourself out there. This is your chance to make an impression and show them how special you are."

I smile weakly. I'm one of sixteen girls and ranked in twelfth place. I don't feel so special.

"I'm serious," she adds. "And besides, you look incredible."

I do like how I look. I'm dressed in a sparkly pale blue dress. My brown hair is curled in loose waves down my back. I've got makeup on—red lips, black lashes framing my brown eyes with blue sparkles across the lids, and white shimmery dust on my collarbone. Nova snuck in at the last minute to apply those last two touches. She even sprayed me with perfume that smells like a perfect summertime night, making me hope for better days ahead. Even though we're all dressed up, none of the other girls got her added touch.

We dock, are loaded onto a bus, and a few minutes later are dropped off in front of the most gorgeous building I've ever laid eyes on. It's three stories tall with white columns all across the front. A monument outside of it reads "Hibernian Hall, established 1840," and I smile because I actually read those words without trouble.

"At least we're going to be indoors," I say to Joanna.

"No kidding. It gets cold and dark fast in January,"

she agrees. She lets out a little puff of breath that instantly crystalizes, proving her point.

We're herded inside and are met with a blast of welcoming heat. I gasp as I take in the decorations. This place is even prettier inside than it is on the outside.

Huge pine trees are set up with tiny snowflakes and silvery blue wolf ornaments hanging from them. In our village we celebrate Christmas, but not here. The day came and went just like any other. But this feels like Christmas, even though the decorations are all blue and white. We girls are released to the ballroom, and I stroll through the trees, running my fingertips against the prickly needles. Maybe tonight won't be so bad.

"Your dress matches the decorations." Ryne's familiar scent of spicy earth surrounds me, and I clench my teeth. I tell myself that he is the last man I want to talk to, but I know it's a lie. I don't turn around, but I feel the heat of Ryne's body close to mine. I shouldn't, but I want to lean back against him and feel his arms around my waist.

"I'm sorry about Faye," he whispers, his breath caressing my ear. "I had to throw my father off your scent."

I clutch at my dress, and a weight lifts off my heart. He was protecting me. Why would he do that? Part of me doesn't want to believe him, but the bigger part desperately does. "Is your father here tonight?" I brush my fingers along the edges of a snowflake decoration, and glitter sticks to them.

"No," he breathes, resting one hand on my hip. "You look beautiful. I have half a mind to take you as my mate tonight."

I can't help it. I spin and stare into his gorgeous blue eyes. They're framed by his dark lashes. His black hair hangs around his cheeks, begging for my hands to run through it. I don't understand this man.

"Why would you do that?"

He chuckles and runs a finger down my cheek. "You are clueless as to how captivating you are, aren't you?" He sighs. "As much as I want to, I can't. It will not be easy watching you go with one of my betas, but it will be better than the mating house."

"Just not Anders. Please. Anyone but Anders."

A frown forms on his lips.

"Did I say something wrong?" I ask.

"I foolishly hoped that maybe you felt the same way about me and would beg me to take you instead. But I guess I was wrong." He steps away and disappears into the crowd. I stand there for a moment feeling thoroughly confused. If I had begged him to take me, would he have? He isn't the type to want a desperate female. Or maybe he is, and I completely misread him.

"You know, I heard about your sister." Faye's familiar drawl grates on my ears. I don't respond, still watching Ryne's retreating back. "She was killed because they found out she whored herself out before they came for her. Beta wives are meant to be virgins. You must be so ashamed."

Anger bubbles up in my chest. I spin around to face her. "That is not true. She was killed because Anders is an asshole who couldn't keep his hands to himself, and she wasn't taking it."

Faye let out a laugh. "Likely story. How long did it take you to make that up? I bet that's why Ryne likes you."

"Shut your mouth, Faye."

"Oh honey, you only wish I'd shut up because you know I'm speaking the truth. Deep down, you know Ryne only likes you because he's hoping you're a slut too." She pokes my chest with each word that follows. "Just. Like. Willow."

Fury burns behind my eyes, and I slap her across the face without thinking. Hearing her say Willow's name was too much. She holds a hand to her face, her eyes wide.

"You little bitch." She reaches over and pulls my hair so hard that my eyes water. I scratch at her arms, but she doesn't let go. I stomp down on her exposed toe with my heel, and she screeches. She lets go but lunges for me, her hands flapping.

This is not the combat I know, but I can't manage to punch her when she's thrashing at me with nails and teeth. Instead, I grab at a flap on her dress and pull. It makes a satisfying ripping noise. She gasps and tackles me. My back hits the floor hard, but I manage to hold my head up so it doesn't crack on the floor. I struggle underneath her but can't move very well in my dress. I scratch at her face and yank her hair out of its careful updo. She claws at my dress and then goes for my hair too.

She's suddenly lifted away, and everything stills. A livid Madame Delphine towers over me. Grady holds a struggling Faye back, and Joanna helps me up. One strap of my dress is torn away, and there is a rip from the bottom clear up to my thigh.

Ryne stands a little ways away, his arms crossed and lips twitching. He thinks this is funny! Madame Delphine does not. Her face turns as purple as a Christmas plum, and she looks back and forth between us. Faye calms down, and Grady lets go of her.

"Never in all my years of running Drayton Hall have I seen such a spectacle. Fighting is never allowed among my girls, and to do so at such a public event is unforgivable." She swallows hard. "I'm sorry, but I can't see any other way to proceed. You will each lose fifty points."

My shoulders fall. Fifty points is a lot. Now it's going to be even harder for me to work my way up the board, but at least I made it for tonight.

Faye smirks at me. "When will the points be taken, Madame?"

"Immediately."

My world closes in around me in slow motion.

"So does that mean that Poppy drops to the bottom of the board right now?"

Madame Delphine's face falls for just a second before responding. She straightens her shoulders, avoiding my eyes. "Yes."

Bile rises in my throat, and I seek out Ryne's gaze once again. He's not laughing anymore.

Faye presses on. "So Poppy is heading for the mating house? She's got to be at the bottom of the list now."

Madame Delphine purses her lips. "Yes. I suppose that would be the case. I'm so sorry, Poppy." Her face is ashen. "The most disappointing part is that you did this to yourself."

After all that hard work, my worst nightmare has come true.

CHAPTER 29

JOANNA CLUTCHES AT MY ARM. "But you can't do that. She was fourth from the bottom when we left the house."

Madame Delphine sniffs. "How did you know that? The points weren't posted today."

I open and close my mouth, wanting to reveal what Nova told me but knowing that I can't get her in trouble. Besides, it would be pointless now anyway.

"Never mind." Madame Delphine shakes her head. "Whatever the score was, it was before that despicable display. I hope the rest of you girls will learn from Poppy's mistake."

I want to defend myself and explain how Faye goaded me into it, but I don't because it won't do any good. Fifty points for Faye just bumped her to the middle of the board, but I'm a goner. When we left tonight, everything looked so hopeful. And now, it's all gone. This isn't fair.

I glance around, taking in the crowd of elegantly dressed party guests. They're all gaping at me. It's the full moon, so not every beta is here, but it certainly feels like it. And the ones that are married have brought their wives along. The women are nothing like me. They're polished and perfect and glaring down their noses in my direction. They must think I'm pathetic and want me sent away this very minute. There's not an ounce of compassion among them.

Madame Nova appears at my side, gripping my elbow. "Come on, let's get you cleaned up."

I jerk out of her arms. "Why? She just started what they'll finish." I nod to the pack of wolves who now all eye me hungrily. They didn't know who was headed for the mating house when they arrived tonight. Now I'm fresh meat.

She drags me away from the crowd anyway, and Joanna grips my other arm. We enter a bathroom that is designed in entirely cream marble and warm lights. Madame Nova grabs a few fluffy white hand towels and wets them in the sink. Joanna gets to work on my hair.

I catch sight of myself in the mirror. I'm a mess. My hair sticks out in all directions. Dirt and blood cover my face and shoulders.

"I need you to listen to me," Nova says, each word a careful directive.

I jerk my eyes down to meet hers.

"I'm going to talk to Nico and ask him to speak to Ryne on your behalf. We need to see about getting you sent to either the Pennsylvania Alley or Church Street mating houses. Church street would be best, but all the women want in there, so it's harder to get into. Once you are there, ask for Flora."

"At which one?"

"Doesn't matter. It's a code word for help, and the girls there will take care of you."

"How are any of the mating houses better than others? Seems like they would all be terrible."

Nova snorts. "Each house has a reputation, and the men go to the ones that cater to their needs. Broad Street is the worst. If you get word that they are sending you there, run. Death is better than the horrors they'll inflict on you there."

"Church Street is the best because it feels more like dating. The men that go there want the girls to want them, so they rarely take a girl without her consent. A few girls there have long-standing relationships with warrior betas, and some are even monogamous. Pennsylvania Alley is similar, but it's not quite as good."

Panic builds in my chest. I don't want to do any of it. I want to run right now, but that means Evan and my parents would die, and I don't want that either. I rub my sweaty palms along my ripped dress but find them too shaky.

I bend over, breathing hard. "I can't do this."

"You can, and you will. Poppy, you are strong, and this won't break you. Now, you have to go back out there and pretend like everything is fine. That is the life of a claimed woman. I'm going to find Nico and see what I can do for you." She puts both of her hands on my shoulders and forces me to look at her. "Don't let them know they've gotten to you. If they sense weakness, it's all over. Be strong, Poppy."

Joanna grips my arm and leads me out of the bathroom and back to the party.

I don't feel strong at all.

There's dancing, but it's a blur—the music, the couples, the laughter, the smells, the food, the enjoyment—none of it matters anymore. And then I'm dancing too, being passed from beta to beta, but it's only my body on the dance floor because my mind is elsewhere. I don't hear what they say or register much of what's happening.

I look up to find that I'm in the arms of the man whose fault it is that I'm here tonight. Anders smiles down at me with a sinister grin and brings his lips to my ears. "I had hoped that you would be my wife, but this way I get you earlier. I'll be sure to find you at your new mating house."

I don't say a word. I can't. His hand on my back slips lower and lower, but before I react the same way Willow did—and I should, death would be better than what I'm about to do—Grady cuts in and pulls me close.

"Are you okay?" he whispers.

I shake my head.

"I wish I could say something that would make this better, but there's nothing to say. I can, however, keep you from having to dance with creepy men."

I clutch at him, grateful for this one small mercy. "Thank you."

We fall into an easy silence as we dance. All I can think about is going to the mating house tonight. I'm terrified they are going to send me to Broad Street.

The king may not be here at the dance, but he promised he would find me at the mating house, that he would have me before his son. And if Nova is right about different houses having different reputations, then he will make sure I am sent to one where he can abuse me all he wants. Nova said she'll have Nico try to help me out, but I can't cling to the false hope.

I glance over to where Faye is dancing with Anders. She's smiling at him as if she hasn't a care in the world. The wound on her cheek healed this week. She said she wished it were me who had been beat up, and now it will be. I know she is awful, but I never thought she would do something like this. She goaded me with fake gossip about Willow, and like an idiot, I fell for it. Now she's middle of the board, and I'm done for. At least Ivy is probably saved, though I have no doubt Callista is at the bottom with me. I look over to where Ivy is dancing with Justin. She's a follower, going along with whatever her friends want. She's like a pliable clay in Justin's hands. Too bad he's not interested. His eyes aren't even on her. They're on Faye as she laughs at something Anders says.

Faye will end up a beta wife if she doesn't somehow nab Ryne. And just because Ivy escaped the mating house this time doesn't mean she'll survive the next cut in three months or the two after that. I may even see her at a mating house if we get sent to the same one.

Where will I be in three months? With any luck, I'll already be pregnant and waiting it out in the birther's house. I always wanted a family. Being a mother one day was a given. A fact of life. Now I'll be a womb and nothing more.

A tear slips down my cheek, and Joanna is instantly at my side, leading me away from the watchful eyes. I catch sight of Ryne. He's staring at me with the same kind of intensity he used in his battles. Is he angry at me? I think so. Well, I'm angry at myself too.

We escape the massive ballroom and wind through a few back hallways until we end up in a kitchen. The staff is busy refilling the trays of food and sending them back out with the servers. There are no human men here. Only older women, the ones who aren't of child-bearing age anymore. They've all been in my shoes, and they look at me with knowing pity but don't say a word as Joanna leads me to the sink and helps me mop up my tears.

At last, she hugs me. "I'm sorry," she whispers in my ear, so quietly that nobody else can possibly hear. "Nova will get you sent to a good mating house, you'll see. Just go along with it and keep a low profile. Wait for a message from me. I am going to get you out of there as soon as—"

I step back and ask bitterly, "When are you going to give this up? There's nothing you can do to save me."

"I'm serious," she continues, looking around her to make sure nobody is listening. She pulls me back into another hug and whispers low again. "You don't understand. I'm part of a network of people who are fighting this system from within, and we're going to help you. Remember to ask for Flora." She lets me go.

I blink at her, a million questions swirling in my mind. She shakes her head once. It's not safe to talk about it. Not here. Probably not anywhere. But it all makes sense now. I wish she had trusted me with this information sooner. I hope it's real. I hope she can help me. And hope is all I have to cling to. There's nothing else left.

"Where is she?" A male voice rips through the room. Joanna and I jump.

Nico appears with Ryne on his heels. His hair is disheveled, and his eyes are mad with panic. He turns to us. "Have you seen Nova?" His voice pleads.

I frown because I thought she was going to find him.

"We'll help you look for her," Joanna chimes in. "She's probably just in the bathroom or something. She helped Poppy clean up after the fight."

"No." Nico shakes his head. "We looked everywhere. We've turned this place upside down. The kitchen is the last place to check." He looks around helplessly, and the women scurry out of his way as he starts tearing through the cupboards, as if somehow Nova could be in one. It's irrational. But then again, so is love.

Ryne spins him around and forces Nico to look at him. "Pull yourself together."

Nico's face falls. "But she was supposed to become my mate."

"I know. But she probably got cold feet. You gave her a year and then drastically upped the timeline. I'm sure she's back at home waiting for you. You need to give her more time. She's been through a lot with the mating house and everything."

"I thought she loved me."

"She does. I've seen you two together, and I know she does. But she just needs a little more time to get used to things. You owe her that."

Nico nods, but he keeps his shoulders slumped, avoiding looking at any of us.

Ryne meets my eyes. "It's time. Madame Delphine is probably looking for you two. I'm going to pretend I didn't see you trying to run away again."

Joanna scoffs. "We aren't trying to run away. Poppy just needed a place to cry, you asshole."

He gives another stiff nod.

"Nico, do you know what mating house I'll be sent to?" I have to know.

He and Ryne exchange a guarded look and then leave without answering. My heart rate quickens as we follow them back to the ballroom. My feet feel like they're filled with lead. Joanna and I are going up on a stage with the rest of the claimed, and then once again I will be forced from my home and taken to a place I do not want to go.

I wonder how long it will be before the others join me, but there are many mating houses. Maybe I'll never see any of them again.

Even though I tried to walk slowly, before I know it, we're up on a stage with Ryne standing several paces in front of us, howling at his betas. It seems so strange to see them acting so uncivilized when they are dressed in tuxedos. But there's nothing civilized about them. They are monsters, all of them.

Joanna clutches my hand. We stand in the middle of the claimed women. I wish I could stand in the back, but there is no back. We are lined up, all in full view of the betas before us.

"Tonight, two of the claimed will join the mating houses. Would you like to meet the girls who will serve at your pleasure?" Ryne asks.

Bile rises in my throat, but I swallow it down. Nothing will save me now, and vomiting in front of all of them would just be embarrassing.

Ryne walks the line and pulls out Callista. She whimpers as he leads her to the front of the stage. This is no surprise. We all saw this coming, especially Callista herself.

"Meet Callista. She will be joining the Rainbow Row house."

A cheer goes up in the back of the crowd, no doubt from those who frequent that house. Rainbow Row was not one that Nova mentioned, so I have no idea what that means for her. I can only imagine it's not good. Surely the girls at the bottom of the crop are sent to the least desirable houses.

And then Ryne is in front of me, grabbing my hand and pulling me forward. I squeeze his hand, not wanting to ever let it go. Tonight my whole world will change. I've had months, but I'm still not prepared. I'm not ready to give up my innocence to violent men who will simply move on to the next girl once they've tired of me. I'm not ready for any of this.

Ryne slides his hand across my back, and I hate that I love the way it feels there. "Meet Poppy. She's scheduled to head to Broad Street."

My head begins to spin, and the only thing holding me upright is Ryne's arm. Nova told me to run if they sent me there, but my feet are frozen. I can't move. My life is over.

Ryne squeezes me a little tighter. "But it wouldn't be a Wolf Moon Festival without a few surprises, right?"

The crowd howls again, and my brain races to comprehend what he's saying. He spins me around so I'm facing him and brings both hands to my cheeks. There is something in his eyes that I can't place. Something that looks like fear and longing.

He inches his face closer, and my eyelids flutter shut. Then he presses soft lips against mine, and everything inside me snaps.

CHAPTER 30

IT'S him and me and nobody else. The rest of the world fades away as his lips caress mine. He presses closer, fingers clawing into my hair, mouth demanding in the sweetest way possible, and I lose myself. This is so much more than simply lips against lips. It's his soul exploring mine. It's each of us having a missing piece that we didn't even realize was lost until this very moment—the moment that we find that piece in each other.

I find myself in him.

How can that be? He's the alpha of the Carolina Pack. He's powerful and tortured and sinful and everything wrong for me. I'm just a simple farm girl who wasn't even supposed to come here. But I am here, and I can't deny this feeling.

It's not attraction or lust. I don't know if it's love, but it feels like it could be.

It's fate. Of that, I am absolutely certain.

Too soon, Ryne releases me and stares deep into my eyes. His are like a terrible storm finally parting to reveal the clear blue sky. He has no more questions about us either. He feels it too—knows it too.

We're fated mates.

My heart leaps for joy, and I can't help but smile. "It's you," I whisper softly.

He frowns, breaks our gaze, and turns back to the crowd. There are no cheers. It's dead quiet. Everyone is staring, suspicion and confusion evident on their faces. I lick my bottom lip, just to taste him one last time, and realize everyone is watching me too. I'm sure they saw everything and are judging me. My feelings are laid out as if my chest has been ripped open, and my wild heart is on display for everyone to sneer at. Who am I to be fated to Ryne? I'm nobody to them. But maybe they don't matter. Maybe all that matters is what Ryne thinks. My cheeks burn, and I sink behind his broad shoulders, trying to hide myself.

"That was fun." He laughs the kiss off. "You all know the only way a claimed can be saved from the mating house on a festival night is a kiss from the alpha. I don't think the girls knew that though."

A gasp goes out among the girls, and the crowd chuckles knowingly. We definitely did *not* know this rule. And I don't understand. I thought Ryne kissed me because he wanted me. I thought we were going to be together now. Didn't he feel what I did? Aren't we fated? Maybe it's both—maybe he saved me because we're fated.

The betas don't say a word, so Ryne continues. "I've never used it before, even though my father loved using that particular loophole to get the ladies all worked up on festival nights." He smiles ruefully, and the crowd chuckles again. Many of them must have known the previous alpha before he became king. "That said, I think you might want to understand why I saved Poppy." There's a low murmuring of interest among the crowd. "She'd make an excellent beta wife, but there is one beta in particular who practically begged me to save her. Anders, you owe me."

Ryne laughs. The men cheer. The women glare. And Anders grins wickedly.

Wait—Ryne only kissed me to save me for Anders? If I'm fated to Ryne, then surely I'm to be *his* wife. But maybe we're not actually fated. Maybe I made the whole thing up like pathetic, wishful thinking. But no. That can't be. I know what I felt. So why didn't Ryne feel it too? I thought for sure that he had when he looked at me, but he did frown . . .

My eyes burn. I can't help it. He rejected me and is pawning me off on Anders. The man who killed Willow. The man he *knows* I want nothing to do with. This is nearly as painful as watching my sister die all over again because I know that every time I have to look at Anders is another time I have to be reminded of her death. I can't stand it. I need to get out of here. My hands start to shake, and my vision blurs with tears.

"But I didn't just do this because Anders asked." Ryne goes on. "I did it because Poppy deserves it. She's the best fighter of the bunch and the most physically fit. She's innocent, pure, and obviously beautiful." That one gets a few whoops. "Yes, she needs to work on some of her other skills, but she's also humble. There are several instances where she should have earned more points but never demanded them, not as some of her fellow claimed have done."

His gaze lands on Faye for a long moment, and she squares her shoulders. Did Faye demand more points? I wouldn't put it past her.

"For example," he continues, "what many of you don't know is that one of her classmates turned into a lycan during a full moon a few months ago." The crowd grows uneasy at this news. "When the other girls tried to protect themselves, she did the opposite. She tried to save the other claimed and put herself in mortal danger. That proves that she has the kind of bravery my men need in a wife."

The crowd shifts gears, and they cheer again. It shakes me from my heartbreak, and I give them a little smile. Their applause is for *me*. I can hardly believe it.

"Now I know many of you men have been waiting patiently for new recruits, so our third-place woman will be joining the Broad Street Mating House. Poppy will continue on at Drayton House with the others. Anders, I expect you to make sure my kiss was not given in vain. You treat this girl right, do you hear me?" Anders gives me a smile, and I want to gag. Does this mean I have to be his wife at the end of all of this? It's pretty clear Anders has made his intentions known. At least I'm not going to the mating house today, but the thought of Anders has me in knots.

"Ivy," Ryne continues, "please come forward."

Madame Delphine appears at my side and ushers me off the stage without a word. Reality sinks in as the crowd parts to let us through. Ivy is standing with her friends, her mouth open and her head shaking. She sends a pleading look at Faye, but Faye shrugs and steps back.

"I tried to help you," Faye hisses. "You should be grateful I sacrificed points for you."

Leave it to Faye to make this about her.

"That isn't fair," Ivy gasps. Someone pushes her out into the center of the floor. She stumbles over her silver gown before righting herself. She's all alone, but not for long. Two men come for her. "No! I'm third! Poppy can't do that."

"Poppy didn't," one of the men snaps. "Our alpha did."

"Then your alpha is wrong!"

"Don't you dare question our alpha," he growls.

Brown fur flashes over his arm, ripping open his suit jacket. He's about to shift, to attack, but he gathers himself together and stays in his human form.

She shakes her head until her hair pops free of one of the clips. It falls in a long dark curl down her back, and the other man snatches it between his fingers, lifting it to his nose. These are betas I don't know, betas who might even be married already, but there's a cruelty inside of them that is unmistakable.

"Get off me!" Ivy screams. It's the first time I've seen any real fire from the girl, but it's too late. She fights with her nails and teeth when the men grab her and haul her from the ballroom. I don't blame her for defending herself, but she shouldn't fight them. Fighting will attract violent men to her bed. She'll live to regret showing this side of herself to all these betas. That's if she lives through the Broad Street house at all. I suddenly wish I'd have sat the girls down and explained what I knew about the mating houses—competition be damned. Hopefully, Ivy and Callista will be pregnant with a stranger's baby by the next full moon. What an awful thing to hope for.

Guilt rakes through me. Ivy is right. This isn't fair. But I'm also so relieved that it's her and not me, and that alone makes the guilt even worse. I can't allow myself to hold on to it. It's misplaced guilt. It should be anger, and it should be directed right back at the men who created the mating houses in the first place.

Madame Delphine keeps a tight arm around my shoulders. "Come, ladies, it's time to get out of here. The real festivities begin at midnight, and it's no place for a lady."

I don't know what's about to happen, but we've left Callista and Ivy in the men's clutches. They will not be the same after tonight.

We are led outside, Madame Delphine staying at my side. There are guards everywhere, most in their wolf forms and way more than when we first arrived. I gaze up at the full moon and shiver. It feels like we're risking so much being outside right now. I feel exposed and vulnerable, and I just want to be safe. I don't know if that will ever be possible again. The wolves walk with us on all sides, but it doesn't help. Somewhere in the distance, one of them howls at the moon. For a second, I imagine it's a lycan's screech and not a wolf's call.

Joanna keeps pace with me. "Are you okay?"

I shake my head.

"At least you're not in a mating house."

"Is that any better than being promised to Anders?"

"It's not promised, exactly. There's no guarantee."

"Um, I'm pretty sure he called dibs tonight, and Ryne helped him do it."

"Be grateful, child," Madame Delphine says emphatically. "This is infinitely better than where you were headed. I know you don't like Anders, and I know he killed your sister, but one cruel man is better than hundreds. Trust me."

I don't say anything because she would know. She was the wife of likely the cruelest one of them all. But the thought of sharing kisses or a bed with Anders fills me with dread.

The thought of sharing kisses with anyone but Ryne feels wrong at this point. I shake my head. I must've imagined that connection. He was just a good kisser. I'll move past that kiss. And hopefully I'll be able to find a way out of the marriage with Anders. Just because Ryne wants me to marry him doesn't mean another beta can't claim me. I'll just have to work extra hard to make that happen.

Nova will help me get Justin. I wish she'd have stayed instead of going home early tonight, but I don't blame her. The festival probably brought up a lot of bad memories. And if her disappearing tonight means she's not ready to accept Nico as her husband, then he needs to respect that. But I know she loves him. She'll be his wife by the end of the year. And in the meantime, she can be my friend and ally at the house. The others may want to push me off on Anders, but I'm certain Nova will be on my side.

Once we reach the path back to the boat, Madame Delphine lets go of me, and Joanna takes my hand. Grady jogs up next to us. "Look at that, you girls get to stay together after all. You'll both be beta wives."

Joanna scowls at him but doesn't say anything. We reach the river, but the boat isn't there yet. The girls all mingle among themselves, but I wander down to stare out over the water. It's dark, and lights from the surrounding buildings cast an eerie wash of color over the whole thing. There are two moons now, the one in the sky and the one reflecting in the water.

I have no idea what the future looks like. Does this mean I'll no longer have to worry about points if Ryne can kiss me at festivals to keep me reserved for Anders? Is the threat of the mating house a thing of the past?

Something floats out in the river just below me, and I creep closer to get a better look. A log. My voice catches in my throat. That's not a log. It's a body.

"Help," I finally scream and scramble down the embankment. "Help!"

Footsteps pound behind me, but I splash into the water. It's a woman wearing a pretty pink gown. No. No. This can't be happening.

I flip the body over and let out a whimper. Nova is staring up at me with very bloodshot, very dead eyes.

I hear splashes behind me, but I don't move. I just cling to the dead body of a woman I've come to love. She cared for me in a way that the other house mothers did not.

Grady reaches past me and takes Madame Nova into his arms. "Come on, Poppy," he whispers. Nico stands on the shore, his face a mask of horror. Grady reaches him before I do and hands him the body. Nico lets out a gut-wrenching cry. It transforms into a heartbroken howl, and the other men join in. We girls just stand there, staring, broken, disbelieving.

How did she die? She wouldn't have killed herself. She truly cared for Nico. It could've been an accident, but I doubt it. Someone killed her. But why? I trudge back up the embankment. All the girls stand there, clutching at each other.

Joanna throws her arms around me and hugs tightly. It's a hug that reminds me of Willow, and my tears break free for the third time tonight. But I'm not weak for crying. I'm strong for facing the truth of our situation. I whisper quietly into her ear. "If you and Nova"—my voice breaks a little at her name—"are part of some kind of resistance group, then I need to be a part of it too."

She steps back, nodding once, her eyes shining with pride and grief and a million things unsaid. She takes my hands in hers. I'm not sure how I'm going to make a difference. Who am I? I'm only one girl. One *human* girl.

But I'll find a way.

To Be Continued in Book 2...

Dear Reader,

Oh my goodness, did you see that ending coming? Because we sure didn't! Poppy and Ryne's story is just beginning so don't forget to grab book two on our series page. New World Shifters Series: www.amazon.com/gp/product/B09314CXNY

Also, we've got a surprise for you. That kiss at the end left us wanting to know more so we wrote the scene in Ryne's point of view as well. Do you want it? (We know the answer to that question is yes.) To gain access to the file, you'll have to join both of our Facebook groups. Here is the link for Nina's group: www.facebook.com/groups/ninasreadingparty and Kim's group: www.facebook.com/groups/KimberlyLothReleaseParty. Happy reading!

If you loved this book, please leave a review and don't forget to tell your friends. Help us spread the word! www.amazon.com/dp/B092W9TG6Q

We weren't quite sure what would happen when we wrote together and we were both surprised to find it was magic. This has been one of our all time favorite books to write.

Love you guys! Thanks for taking this journey with us.

XO,

Kim and Nina

ABOUT THE AUTHOR: NINA WALKER

Nina Walker is a USA Today and Amazon Top 100 Bestselling author. She lives near the beautiful red mountains of southern Utah with her family. She writes across multiple fantasy genres and loves metaphysical magic systems, forbidden love interests, and unexpected plot twists. Nina also co-writes romantic comedy under the pen name, Grace Costello.

Learn more at www.ninawalkerbooks.com & follow her shenanigans on Instagram or TikTok @ninabelievesinmagic.

For early access opportunities and bonus gifts, please join her Facebook reader group "Nina's Reading Party."

Book Nine: www.kimberlyloth.com/CODChronicles9

Book Ten: www.kimberlyloth.com/CODChronicles10

Circus of the Dead (Young Adult Romantic Thriller)

Circus of the Dead Book 1: www.kimberlyloth.com/CircusOfTheDead1

Circus of the Dead Book 2: www.kimberlyloth.com/CircusOfTheDead2

Circus of the Dead Book 3: www.kimberlyloth.com/CircusOfTheDead3

Circus of the Dead Book 4: www.kimberlyloth.com/CircusOfTheDead4

Circus of the Dead Boxed Set

The Thorn Chronicles (Young Adult Paranormal)

Midnight Angel: www.kimberlyloth.com/midnight

Destroyer Angel: www.kimberlyloth.com/destroyer

Fallen Angel: www.kimberlyloth.com/fallen

Guardian Angel: www.kimberlyloth.com/guardian

The Thorn Chronicles Boxed Set

Michigan Millionaires (Sweet Romance Series)

Lukas: www.kimberlyloth.com/lukas

Jamie: www.kimberlyloth.com/jamie

Hayden: www.kimberlyloth.com/hayden

Adam: www.kimberlyloth.com/adam

Tristan: www.kimberlyloth.com/tristan

Conner: www.kimberlyloth.com/conner

Blake: www.kimberlyloth.com/blake *coming fall 2021

Stella and Sol (Young Adult Fantasy)

God of the Sun: www.kimberlyloth.com/sun

Prince of the Moon: www.kimberlyloth.com/moon

King of the Stars: www.kimberlyloth.com/stars

Queen of the Dawn: www.kimberlyloth.com/dawn

Stella and Sol Box Set

Sons of the Sand (Young Adult Paranormal)

The Smoking Lamp: www.kimberlyloth.com/smoking

The Blazing Glass: www.kimberlyloth.com/blazing

The Glowing Sands: www.kimberlyloth.com/glowing

The Exploding Sky: www.kimberlyloth.com/exploding

YA Contemporary Fiction

Bittersweet: www.kimberlyloth.com/bittersweet

Something About Forever: www.kimberlyloth.com/forever

ABOUT THE AUTHOR: KIMBERLY LOTH

Kimberly Loth has lived all over the world. From the isolated woods of the Ozarks to exotic city of Cairo. She currently resides in the beautiful Sugar Creek in southern Missouri, with her husband and her adorable dog Maisy.

She's been writing for twelve years and is the author of the Amazon bestselling series The Dragon Kings. In her free time she volunteers at church, reads, and travels as often as possible.